HALFHYDE ON THE AMAZON

St Vincent Halfhyde, commanding the steamer *Taronga Park*, is under orders to leave Liverpool for the Amazon River. His passenger is a senior British diplomat charged with a delicate mission to Brazil, where the German Emperor is believed to be establishing a naval base from which to harass British shipping in the event of war. Halfhyde's voyage is plagued with clashes of personalities, with bad weather ... and murder. But when Detective Inspector Todhunter is embarked to sail with the ship, Halfhyde is unclear whether the policeman's investigations are just confined to finding a killer.

HALFHYDE ON THE AMAZON

Philip McCutchan

A Lythway Book

CHIVERS PRESS
BATH

First published in Great Britain 1988
by
George Weidenfeld & Nicolson Limited
This Large Print edition published by
Chivers Press
by arrangement with
George Weidenfeld & Nicolson Limited
and in the USA with
St Martin's Press, Inc
1990

ISBN 0 7451 1164 5

British Library Cataloguing in Publication Data

McCutchan, Philip, 1920–
    Halfhyde on the Amazon.
    I. Title
    823'.914 [F]

ISBN 0–7451–1164–5

DEC (1) '92

HALFHYDE ON THE AMAZON

CHAPTER ONE

'I am not a happy man,' Halfhyde said.

'Oh, for God's sake!'

He looked down at the girl by his side, holding fast to his arm and looking no more pleased with the prospect of the Mersey drizzle than he was himself. 'Good Liverpool weather,' he said drily as they emerged from Lime Street railway station. He hailed a cab: even the horse, beneath its waterproof back-covering, looked desolate; likewise the elderly cabby on the box.

Victoria said, 'You ought to be bloody pleased, mate, you know that? About to take over the bloody *Taronga Park* again—' She broke off and looked penitent: Halfhyde was always reprimanding her about over-use of the Australian adjective. 'Sorry, mate. It just bloody slips out . . . and you're enough to make anyone swear. Just because you—'

'Just because I lost a ship.'

'That was bloody *weeks* ago—and it wasn't your fault. All the way back from bloody South Africa . . . all the way up the South Atlantic, moan—'

'Don't keep the horse waiting,' Halfhyde said coldly, and lifted her bodily into the cab. 'The poor creature wants its oats,' he added as he deposited her in a corner amid a musty smell of

1

old leather. She giggled suddenly and snuggled up to St Vincent Halfhyde's hard, bony frame. The cabby whipped up the horse and the animal ambled away towards the docks, along Lime Street and Water Street, past the massive buildings housing the shipping companies that gave the port of Liverpool its meaning and its great prosperity—tall, grey stone edifices to commercial enterprise and a race of men who took British cargoes across all the world's seas to keep Britain great and to sustain the far-flung Imperial armies and navies standing guard over Queen Victoria's Pax Britannica. Today those buildings were bleak, rain-washed, depressing as Liverpool so often was; and in line with Halfhyde's own thoughts.

No shipmaster had ever liked losing a command and never mind the cause, the chicanery and the guns behind the criminals who had brought about the end of the square-rigger *Glen Halladale* whilst she had been running her easting down from Durban to Cape Leeuwin. *Force majeure*—and in the finish a case of the gunmen being hoist with their own petard. There had been satisfiaction in that, at all events.

The cab rumbled over the cobbles and halted at the dock gate. Halfhyde identified himself to the policeman on duty.

'Master of the *Taronga Park*.'

The constable saluted and the horse moved

on through the drizzle. Grey and dismal; stevedores with split sacks over heads and shoulders in an effort to remain as dry as possible; cranes and gantries, bales being swung into and out of holds at the loading and discharging berths; the port as busy as ever, a forest of masts and yards from the sailing ships, the windjammers in from Australian waters or bound away to Cape Horn and Chile, thin funnels poking up from the steamers that were driving the real ships off the seas. Halfhyde felt a pang, once again, at the loss of the *Glen Halladale*, at the fact he was going back to steam, even though the old *Taronga Park* was his own ship—his own ship as both owner and master. He told himself the truth: that the *Glen Halladale*, under charter to the Admiralty, had been no more than an interlude, a temporary appointment brought about by the exigencies of the war against the Boers in South Africa while the *Taronga Park* had lain idle under care and maintenance in the port of Liverpool, the government requisition to carry stores to Cape Town having never, in the event, been put into commission.

ii

On the previous day, St Vincent Halfyde had attended at the Admiralty in London to render his personal report of events in South Africa and to receive the congratulations of a starchy

3

rear-admiral in a frock-coat and wing-collar.

'You acquitted yourself well, Halfhyde. I would, of course, expect no less of an officer once of the Queen's ships—on that score, I consider you were a loss to the service. However, that's in the past. Now we must look to the future.'

Halfhyde gave a short laugh. 'Is there to be a future, sir?'

'You still have your own ship, the *Taronga Park*. Tell me, what do you propose to do with her, Halfhyde?'

Halfhyde shrugged. 'Find myself a cargo, sir, to anywhere that's offering.'

'Not an easy task. Even for steamers there's a lot of competition for cargoes and you yourself have not the experience of commercial ships to compete in a tender against masters and owners who've known the ropes for half a lifetime. Besides which, your ship is small. That is a restricting factor, is it not?'

Halfhyde admitted that it was. 'But I shall not be idle, I shall not—'

'No, no. I know your reputation, Halfhyde. I know you're a man of resource and enterprise.' There was a meaningful pause. 'But there are better ways, if you're interested—at any rate for one voyage.'

'Are you perhaps referring to another Admiralty charter, sir, this time of the *Taronga Park*?'

4

'Yes,' the rear-admiral answered directly. He had been standing with his hands behind his back, beneath the lifted tails of the frock-coat, staring out of a big window onto Horse Guards Parade across which a colourful troop of Her Majesty's Life Guards was moving. Now he turned suddenly to face Halfhyde and study him intently. He said, 'The Board of Admiralty is faced with a very particular mission, a delicate and important one in the diplomatic field—'

Halfhyde interrupted, a smile on his face now. 'I'm no diplomat, sir. You said you know my reputation. You must know that I am a man of—pointed words.'

'Yes, indeed. Very pointed words to superior officers, and frequently insubordinate during your naval service as a lieutenant. I am told you do not suffer fools at all, let alone gladly.'

Halfhyde inclined his head. 'As I said—no diplomat.'

'But you will not be required to act in that capacity.'

The rear-admiral moved across to his desk, an immense affair occupying an entire corner of the room. He pulled open a drawer and brought out a chart. He beckoned Halfhyde over. Halfhyde looked down at a chart of the approaches to the River Amazon in Brazil.

The rear-admiral said, 'Strange waters to you, most probably.'

'Strange indeed. I've never approached even the fringes of the river's mouths.'

'No matter—you are a navigator. And the *Taronga Park* is of reasonably shallow draft even when laden. Am I not right?'

'Yes,' Halfhyde said.

'And you shall retain your current commission as a lieutenant of the naval reserve, Halfhyde, but not use your rank unless required to do so.'

'*Shall* retain, sir? Am I being given an order?'

'By no means.' The rear-admiral smiled thinly. 'But you are expected to volunteer.'

'I see.' Halfhyde's tone was curt. 'Does this mean more war?'

'On the contrary, it is to avoid a war. That is, a possible war.'

'You are being mysterious, sir. A war with whom?'

'With the German Empire,' the rear-admiral answered.

iii

Victoria Penn had been waiting for Halfhyde on a bench in St James's Park. It had been one of London's springtime mornings, a day of light and shade and coolness, and the park was peaceful, the rumble of the horse-drawn traffic along the Mall and Birdcage Walk muted and overlaid by the song of birds. She spotted Halfhyde's tall figure swinging along from a

6

distance, saw as he came nearer the set of his jaw, the way he carried his walking-stick sloped against his shoulder like a cutlass, and knew before he spoke that he had important matters on his mind.

'The bastards've nabbed you again,' she said accusingly.

He sat beside her, stretching out long legs. By the water, ducks waddled, peaceful creatures with no worries. Elegant ladies and gentlemen walked past, the latter morning-suited and top-hatted with stiffly starched linen. Halfhyde had seen Victoria's half-envious look: London's upper classes were a far cry from Australia, from the wharves of Sydney Town and the close-clustered humanity to be found down by the Cross where Halfhyde had first encountered her and brought her across the seas in the *Taronga Park*. They were just as far a cry from the hard life of the men who fought the ships around Cape Horn, or ran before the westerlies below the Cape of Good Hope for Fremantle and the passage of the Great Australian Bight to Sydney. Hard days and hard men, with no time for fancy dressing.

'Not talking, eh?' Victoria said. 'For God's sake, mate, what did they say in there?' She waved a hand towards the Admiralty building. 'You've got something on your mind, I know that.'

Halfhyde said, 'I was made an offer.'

7

'What offer?' Large eyes studied his expression and she swept a strand of hair from her face. Then her gaze shifted away from him, her face coloured and she said loudly, 'Bloody bitch!'

Halfhyde lifted an eyebrow. She said, 'That cow that just went past. Looked at me as if I was straight out of the zoo! Reckon I'd—'

'Pay no attention, Victoria. They have no impact on your life or mine and never mind the fancy feathers.' He added, 'We shall soon be at sea again.'

'Well, goodoh! Australia?'

He shook his head. 'Not Australia, although that is to be our official destination when we clear away from the Mersey—and that's between you and me, Victoria, you understand?'

'Reckon I do,' she said doubtfully. 'Bloody secrecy again. It'll bring nothing but bloody trouble, mate, you know that? I reckon we've had enough.'

'But the Admiralty doesn't. And I have to make a living. It's a hard world, Victoria.'

'Dead right it is!' She looked up at him. 'Do they know about me?'

He laughed. 'They could scarcely do otherwise. Your light is obscured by no bushel that I'm aware of! Of course they know about you, and you'll continue aboard my ship. You'll be good cover, Victoria—and as such, useful to

8

Their Lordships.'

She hadn't liked being regarded as cover but was relieved that there had been no objections to her presence aboard the *Taronga Park*. Their Lordships of the Board of Admiralty, she had always understood, were a weird lot, all starch and eyes that looked down noses. Compared with admirals, everyone was as common as dirt. And they didn't like women aboard ships. Halfhyde said she need not have worried: he wouldn't have accepted the Admiralty's offer had any objection been raised against the presence of Miss Victoria Penn. On that he was adamant and she believed him. She asked a number of questions as they sat on the bench but he wouldn't answer. Not yet, he said; there was in fact much that he didn't know himself. Once they were away to sea and making down for the Fastnet to take their departure from England, then he might be able to take her into his confidence. By then, he said, he would know more himself. She badgered for a while, then gave it up: St Vincent Halfhyde had an expressive face, and he was growing exasperated. Leaving St James's Park they walked into the Mall where Halfhyde raised his stick for a hansom cab.

'Camden Town,' he said, and handed Victoria in. He called again to the cabby as they turned and came beneath Admiralty Arch, giving the man the address of Mrs Mavitty, in years gone by his landlady during the penurious period of half-pay from the Queen's service, this status having been brought about by his own impetuous temper when dealing with senior officers whom he had considered mentally constipated. So many captains and admirals had considered paintwork and shining brass to be of more importance to the Fleet than accurate gunnery and seaworthiness. Some had gone so far as to have the watertight doors burnished, thus destroying their capabilities, and to have the cable burnished each time an anchor was let go. Halfhyde, son of a farmer from the North Riding, brought up in the down-to-earth purlieus of Wensleydale and Swaledale, had been more than contemptuous of such fussings and had not been slow to say so. In those years of subsequent unemployment on the half-pay list, the good Mrs Mavitty had been his saviour; and he was not the man to forget favours. Hence, each time that he stayed in London, it was to Camden Town that he went for a bed, even though Mrs Mavitty's stern principles caused her to eye Victoria askance, and to fix St Vincent Halfhyde with an eye that said very clearly that whilst under her roof there would be separate bedrooms and no hanky-panky.

Next morning early, it was Euston Station

10

and the train to Liverpool. As, later in the day, the cab rattled into the docks and Halfhyde saw the outline of the *Taronga Park* looming through the Mersey drizzle, his thoughts winged ahead: there would be much to do to prepare the ship for sea; she had been in port for, in seaman's terms, a full due, with, for much of the time, only a watchman aboard. A crew would have to be found and signed on foreign-going articles. He would need good officers and dependable men, and each would be vetted by a naval officer from the Admiralty, who would attend with Halfhyde at the shipping master's office when the signing took place. As cover for the mission, a cargo would be arranged by the Admiralty and taken aboard when the *Taronga Park* shifted to the loading berth. And when the ship was in all repects ready for sea, certain persons as yet unknown to Halfhyde would embark for the voyage to the Amazon River.

Victoria broke into his thoughts.

'Looks sad, I reckon, mate.'

'What does? Liverpool?'

'No, the *Taronga Park*.'

'She'll change. She'll start to live again soon. She's anxious to get to sea again.'

She gave him a sidelong look. 'Like you.'

'I'm a seaman.'

'The only place you feel right, I reckon. Ever going to settle down, are you?'

He grinned. 'Are you thinking of marriage again, Victoria?'

'No,' she said. 'I reckon I gave that up a long while ago. You aren't the marrying sort . . . nor am I, I reckon.'

'Freedom's a great thing,' he said as the cab drew alongside the *Taronga Park* and stopped.

'Dead right. But you know I'll never bloody leave you, mate. God's honour.'

Halfhyde took her hand and squeezed it before he jumped down to lift her gently to the dockside in his arms. She responded with her urchin-like, cheeky grin. His incubus: they would sail the world together, as good as man and wife but with that essential freedom that was in fact a strong bond since Halfhyde would never let her down. She had come into his life by chance back in Sydney, a girl with a sad past, with no friends, no relations that she could find—though there had been brothers and sisters before they had been separated in different orphanages—and, at that time, with no hope. St Vincent Halfhyde had become her hope and that he must continue to be.

Their gear—a couple of dome-topped trunks—deposited on the dock, the cab drove away. Halfhyde called up to the decks of the ship, a strong and carrying voice.

'*Taronga Park* ahoy! Where's the watchman?'

There was no response. Halfhyde called again, cupping his hands. 'There's gear to be brought aboard. Smack it about there.'

No answer; Halfhyde, his face set with anger, was about to set foot on the gangway when a man appeared from the Master's accommodation in the centre island below the bridge, a short, skinny figure in a rather shiny blue serge suit and wearing a seedy bowler hat secured from any possible wind by a toggle connecting its brim to an anchorage set in the jacket's lapel. The starched white collar was high and neck-choking; the face was earnest and was given a sad look by a drooping, grey walrus moustache. Halfhyde gaped in total astonishment as this person peered down at him.

He said, 'Detective Inspector Todhunter, by God! What the devil are you doing here, man?'

'Bless my soul! If it isn't Lieutenant Halfhyde! May I—'

'Captain Halfhyde now, and no longer of Her Majesty's fleet. I am the Master and owner of the *Taronga Park*, Mr Todhunter.'

'Goodness gracious me! The turns of fortune's wheel—I do declare! You'd best come aboard, sir. There's murder been done.'

CHAPTER TWO

Leaving Victoria in charge of the trunks, Halfhyde climbed the gangway and made his way fast along the after well-deck to the ladder at the top of which Detective Inspector Todhunter stood looking down self-importantly. Todhunter had come into the then Lieutenant Halfhyde's life aboard the old battleship *Meridian*, an obsolete warship that was being handed to the Chilean government. Todhunter had been in pursuit of a gentleman of high civilian rank in the Admiralty who had sold secrets to the German Emperor: now Halfhyde wondered about a connection though he could not have said what it might be.

'Well now, Mr Todhunter. Have you left the Metropolitan Police Force?'

'Oh dear me no, Captain Halfhyde! I am still of the Yard. I am here for—for certain purposes. I should say no more than that for the present.' Todhunter gave a cough. 'I wasn't told you would be here, sir, but I am glad to meet again.'

'Thank you, Mr Todhunter. Are you here for the murder?'

'No, sir. That was unexpected. I myself made the discovery when I boarded the ship. There being no answer to my hail, I climbed aboard.

Since no one appeared on deck, I investigated.'

'And you found a body?'

'Indeed I did, Captain Halfhyde, sir, indeed I did. A man with his throat cut. A lot of blood, sir. Very, very nasty. Dead as I explained—'

'Do you know his identity, Mr Todhunter?'

'No, sir. There was nothing on the body to help. Some money and a railway ticket but no documentation.'

'I'd better look for myself,' Halfhyde said. He turned away and climbed on towards the bridge, where he followed the detective inspector into the small chart room just abaft the open platform. A man was lying on the deck, on his back with arms and legs flung wide. Todhunter had not exaggerated about the blood: it was everywhere, and it had dried to a brownish crust. The throat gaped open, red, and swollen with pulpy flesh. The face was a dead white. The skin was smooth, the hands delicate.

Halfhyde said, 'He hasn't the look of a seaman or a stevedore.'

'No, sir. That was my conclusion also.'

'I doubt if he's the watchman.'

'No, sir. Do you suppose the watchman is the guilty party, sir?'

Halfhyde shrugged. 'Your job, Mr Todhunter.'

'I was merely asking your opinion, sir,' Todhunter said in a hurt tone. 'My Chief Super

15

in the Yard—'

'Ah, yes. Is he still the same Chief Super, Mr Todhunter?'

'That he is, sir, yes. A stickler for—'

'So I remember. As to the watchman, who is missing—I suggest we look for another body before we come to any conclusions about him.'

'A good idea,' Todhunter agreed vaguely, looking down at the body. 'I must then alert the dock police, sir. I shall leave you and make my report and return with all necessary equipment and an ambulance to remove the body to the police mortuary as soon as the forensic gentlemen and the measurers have finished. While I am absent I must ask you to kindly touch nothing at all, sir.' Mr Todhunter coughed again. 'It is possible my Chief Super may authorize fingerprints to be looked for—'

'Fingerprints, Mr Todhunter?'

Todhunter said, 'Well, sir, they've been authorized as admissible evidence by the government of India, and—'

'This isn't India, Mr Todhunter. There is no authority here for their use in evidence.'

'Nevertheless they can be of help, Captain Halfhyde.'

'You are a man of advanced thinking, Mr Todhunter.'

Todhunter said modestly, 'I do my best, sir.'

Detective Inspector Todhunter had always worn heavy black boots, Halfhyde recalled as the policeman, before going ashore, clumped about the *Taronga Park* on his search for a second body. The search was thorough but abortive: there were no more bodies and it had to be accepted that the watchman had deserted his post, possibly after committing murder. The man's relief would not be due until six p.m. Had it not been for Todhunter's presumably unexpected visit, and Halfhyde's, the body would not have been found until then.

As Todhunter went ashore to alert the local force, Halfhyde followed him down the gangway to where Victoria was waiting, sitting disconsolately on one of the trunks.

'Well, mate?' she asked, and lowered her voice. 'Who's the little skinny bloke?'

'A flatfoot from Scotland Yard, a detective. You look wet, Victoria—'

'I *am* bloody wet,' she said. She was shivering a little, Halfhyde saw. He picked up one of the trunks, heaved it onto his shoulder and started back up the gangway. Depositing his burden on the deck, he went down again for the second trunk.

He said, 'Get aboard now, Victoria. Go to my cabin and dry off. Nothing's to be touched, so far as it's possible.' He told her about the fingerprints. As she went aboard he shouldered the remaining trunk and carried it up the gangway, dumping it with the other in the after well-deck for the time being, then climbing to his cabin where Victoria, who had gone ahead of him, was looking dismayed.

'Talk about dust and muck, mate!'

'She's been left to the watchmen for a long time. It'll all change when I have a crew aboard. For now, we'll have to pig it.'

'How long for, eh?'

He shrugged. 'A day or two.'

'Should have gone to a hotel, mate.'

'I'm not made of money,' he snapped.

'You'll get paid for—'

'Yes. But I've not been paid yet.'

She sighed. 'Oh, well. Look, all me clothes, they'll be getting wet out there on deck—'

'The trunks are sound and will keep out the weather well enough.' Halfhyde went over to a port and looked out along his decks: all the gear would need to be overhauled, new ropes rove at the derricks before any weights could be lifted, and to carry heavy trunks up near-vertical ladders to his cabin was not possible. He thought about the body above his head: who could the man have been, and why come aboard the *Taronga Park* only to be murdered? And why had the watchman deserted—why had he perhaps murdered a ship visitor? He had to be considered a suspect ... and if he was the culprit then simple financial gain might well be

18

the answer. The body had been well-dressed and the man had looked prosperous. But money had been left on the body . . .

Halfhyde shrugged: Todhunter was the sleuth, not he. He went below to take a further look around the ship while Victoria did her best to make the cabin somewhat more habitable, more like the home it had been and was to be again. Moving about the ship, Halfhyde saw that he was faced with an uphill task. Ships rotted quicky when left in harbour. Money would need to be spent; when the Admiralty officials came aboard they would be approached for an advance on the charter fee as quickly as possible. An attempt had already been made by the rear-admiral to fob him off: first, the charter party documents had to be drawn up and passed by the appropriate department. Red tape abounded in the Admiralty.

The drizzle continued, muting the working sounds of the port. Halfhyde moved along the fore well-deck, past the covered cargo hatch, and climbed the ladder to the fo'c'sle where the anchors were secured at the catheads. The ropes and wires holding the ship to the quayside had the look of having been in position for ever; the rat guards were rusted over and the ropes themselves were fraying in the fairleads. Halfhyde went back down the ladder and as he did so he saw Victoria emerge from the cabin and go to the rail on the port side, the side away from the quay. He continued aft towards the engineers' accommodation in the stern but before he had gone through the door into the alleyway he heard Victoria shout.

'Come here quick, mate!'

'What is it?' He started to move for'ard: there had been panic in the girl's voice.

'Not bloody sure,' she answered, staring down into the murky harbour water. Halfhyde reached her side and followed her pointing finger. He saw what looked like a dark blue bundle, something that might have been no more than a jettisoned coat. Then, as the bundle rolled gently over, he saw the lolling head and the outstretched arms. Death was instantly recognizable. Losing no time he went down at the double to the fore well-deck, where he had seen a grapnel lying idle with a rope attached. Picking this up and coiling the rope in one hand, he went to the bulwarks and cast the grapnel. His first cast was true: the grapnel took the clothing and held. Halfhyde hauled in until the body was close to the ship's side with the water taking its weight, then he turned up the end of the rope around a cleat, removed his jacket, clambered onto the bulwarks, and dived overboard. Having taken the body in his arms, he freed the grapnel and swam, towing his bundle around the bows of the *Taronga Park* to the quayside, where steps cut into the stone gave him easy access. Victoria, almost in

20

hysterics, had been following his movements and as he reached the steps she came down the gangway.

When Halfhyde had the body on the dock wall he saw that it was wearing a seaman's pea-jacket of heavy pilot cloth. The feet were thrust into waterlogged seaboots. With a catch in her voice Victoria said, 'Reckon it's the watchman, right?'

'It's likely,' he said between his teeth. It was a dirty end for any man, and the cause of death was only too obvious: a jagged rip in the back of the jacket, and beneath it a deep gash in the flesh. Somebody had used a knife, and knives were dago objects. By this time a crowd of dockside loafers had gathered round, idly curious: bodies in the Liverpool docks were not too uncommon a find.

Halfhyde got to his feet and addressed the idlers. 'You and you,' he said crisply, 'bring the body aboard my ship.'

One of the men demurred. 'Not so fast, mister. The coppers—'

'I am expecting a detective inspector from Scotland Yard to board shortly. In the meantime, do as I say.' There was the unmistakable voice of authority: the man shrugged, and with his mate picked up the body and moved for the *Taronga Park*'s gangway.

'I don't know, I'm sure, sir.' Detective Inspector Todhunter, back aboard after a little over an hour, pushed his bowler hat to the back of his head and wiped rainwater from his face with a large pocket handkerchief. With him had come the police surgeon and an inspector from the Liverpool force together with three plain-clothes men who busied themselves around the chart room, the ladders leading to the bridge, and in the vicinity of the shore gangway. Todhunter had said they were searching for fingerprints. Even if the law didn't admit the offering of such in evidence, they could nevertheless prove a useful aid to detection. The police surgeon, who estimated that both men had been dead for some ten hours, had taken little time to establish the cause of death in both cases: in the one, a long knife thrust in the back that had penetrated the heart; in the other, a cut throat.

'You are quite certain?' Halfhyde asked sardonically.

The surgeon gave him a sharp look. 'The proper procedures must be observed, Captain Halfhyde. Only a qualified medical practitioner can—'

'Yes, indeed.' Halfhyde turned to Todhunter, asking what conclusions the police had come to; that was when Todhunter said he didn't know, but added a prognostication.

'I'd say, sir, that the person found in the chart room murdered the watchman. Not on deck, I would say, for fear of being seen. He would have lured the man under cover, sir, away from prying eyes.'

'And putting the body overboard, Mr Todhunter? That would not be seen?'

Todhunter said stiffly, 'It seems that in the event it was *not*, Captain Halfhyde, however unlikely a proposition it might sound.'

Halfhyde nodded thoughtfully. The doctor had said ten hours: early morning, shortly after the night-watchman had been relieved ... a dark, rainy morning with the docks not yet astir ... and if the body had been slid down, say, between ship and shore, clear of the fenders that held her off the quayside, and had then drifted ... it was possible enough that no one had seen. However, there was another possibility and Halfhyde voiced it.

He said, 'I told you, I didn't recognize the man. That in itself's not evidence, since he would have been engaged during my absence—but we have to bear in mind that this could be a coincidence. The body could be from another ship, and murdered elsewhere, and drifted down.'

'That I shall find out,' Todhunter said. 'Now we come to the first body. Who murdered *that* man?' He looked round at the others, flipping the pages of his notebook. 'I rather fancy that'll

23

turn out to be the key. Now, Captain Halfhyde, sir, do you intend to remain aboard? I have no objection if you do—'

'Thank you,' Halfhyde said tartly. 'That is indeed what I intend to do.'

'And the lady?'

'And the lady, yes.'

'Very good, sir. Notwithstanding that, I shall leave a police guard, which I shall arrange with the local force—'

'And you yourself, Mr Todhunter? You'll be following your nose, I take it?'

Todhunter said stiffly, 'I shall be reporting to my Chief Super, sir, at the Yard.' Shortly after this all members of the party went back ashore and were conveyed through the docks in a couple of cabs that had lain alongside during their visit, leaving a police constable to guard the gangway, a morose man with a florid face, wearing a cape from which the rain dripped in a continuous stream. He stood, a picture of misery, while Halfhyde and Victoria climbed to the Master's cabin. Halfhyde suggested a cup of tea: knowing there would be no fresh provisions aboard they had brought tea and sugar, milk, eggs and bread to tide them over. In the pantry was an oil stove with fuel to feed it. While tea was brewing there was an interruption: a horse-drawn conveyance pulled up alongside, a vehicle like a small pantechnicon with blank sides and back doors with a heavy iron bar set across in sockets. The constable came up to report that the mortuary van had arrived. The body was fetched from the chart room by four attendants and together with the body from the water was borne down the gangway and incarcerated behind the barred doors.

'Bloody lively tea party,' Victoria said.

It was a depressing night. The drizzle seemed endless. At six p.m. the night-watchman turned up, was admitted past the constable, and, duly warned, climbed to the Master's cabin to report. Like the dead man, his face was new to Halfhyde: he too had been appointed in the Master's absence, and said that the name of the missing watchman was Harry Laws. The night-watchman's name was Platter; Halfhyde told him to hold himself in readiness for a police visit. He would be required to identify the corpse from the water. There were no further visitations that night, but an air of gloom pervaded the ship. Bodies were unpleasant things to welcome an owner and master back aboard. Victoria was restless while Halfhyde, seated at his desk, made lists of matters to be attended to, the first of which would be the signing of a crew: two deck officers, a chief engineer and four juniors, a bosun and carpenter, sixteen seamen, a similar number of oilers and greasers for the engine-room, three stewards and so on. The ship to be provisioned immediately the crew was aboard, coal to be delivered into the bunkers for the boiler ... a hundred and one matters requiring the attention of the Master—and his cash as well. Halfhyde found little sleep after a scratch supper that night and was in no mood for dalliance either, to Victoria's chagrin.

'First Mrs bloody Mavitty and her bloody principles, and now this...'

'I apologise.'

'Oh, piss off!' she said, and turned back to back in the bunk. Next morning Halfhyde was up early, eager to start the day's work. He had been informed at the Admiralty that the ship would be boarded by a naval officer at ten a.m. and that arrangements would have been made with the local shipping office of the Board of Trade for the signing of a full crew one hour later. After a frugal breakfast, Halfhyde paced the deck that ran before his cabin ports, with impatient long strides, back and forth; at ten o'clock sharp, a cab drew up and a thin, dapper man climbed the gangway, spoke briefly to the constable and was saluted aboard with some ceremony. He was brought by the relief watchman to the Master's cabin, where he introduced himself as Commander Wainscott.

'From the Admiralty,' he announced, producing a visiting card.

'As expected,' Halfhyde said. He glanced at Victoria, who was fortunately dressed by this time. 'Miss Penn,' he said to the naval officer.

Victoria said, 'Pleased to meet you.'

'How d'you do.' Commander Wainscott coughed and looked ill-at-ease. The bunk had not yet been made; his thoughts were plainly to be read in his face. Halfhyde rescued him from his embarrassment by saying that he was ready to go ashore to the shipping office and they would not delay.

'Ah, good. I've kept the cab,' Wainscott said. He coughed again and followed Halfhyde out of the cabin, with a half-apologetic backward look at Victoria but no precise goodbye. As they went down the ladder to the after well-deck Halfhyde caught an overloud comment from Miss Penn.

'Bloody pommies...'

Halfhyde and Wainscott embarked in the cab and the horse was whipped up. Wainscott said, 'I was given word in London last night. The local police telegraphed Scotland Yard and a message came to the Admiralty.'

'The murders?'

'Yes.' Commander Wainscott paused. 'I came up to Liverpool on the night train. I've spent the last hour or so with the police—'

'Detective Inspector Todhunter?'

'Yes. And others. The body of the man found in your chart room has been identified. It was I who recognized him. The implications are possibly serious. I say possibly. In fact I would go farther and say that much trouble lies ahead,

27

Captain.'

'In what way?'

Wainscott looked out of the cab windows as they came through the dock gate and didn't answer immediately. Then he said, 'I understand you are not yet in possession of all the facts?'

Halfhyde nodded. 'That's correct. Can you enlighten me, perhaps?'

'In due course, but not at this moment.' Wainscott seemed to go off at a tangent. 'I would like your assurance in regard to Miss Penn, Captain Halfhyde.'

Halfhyde stared. 'I have the Admiralty's permission to keep her aboard. Is that not good enough for you?'

Wainscott said quietly, 'I refer to her integrity. I wish your assurance that she can be fully trusted. When you give me that assurance, you will thereafter be held personally responsible for her actions.'

Halfhyde said, 'You have my absolute assurance, Commander, but I resent its being asked for. The rear-admiral—'

'Yes, yes. But I understand Miss Penn to be of doubtful background. I—'

'Miss Penn,' Halfhyde said with deliberation, his voice and expression cold, 'has the disadvantage in some eyes of having lived in the King's Cross district of Sydney, an unsalubrious area. She was working for the man

Porteous Higgins whose gun-running exploits I was able to bring to an end some while ago—with Miss Penn's assistance willingly given—you'll no doubt have been told of the part played by the *Taronga Park* in bringing Higgins to book. Miss Penn's past is her past, Commander. She is loyal and trustworthy and I repeat what I said to the Admiralty: I shall not sail without her. I trust that is clearly understood.'

'Very well,' Wainscott said. 'I accept your assurance—I apologize for having to ask for it, but there are important issues involved, matters of national security—that much I think you know—'

'Yes. And now perhaps you'll tell me the identity of the dead man.'

Wainscott said, 'Otto Leber.'

'A German?'

'Yes. A German who is *persona non grata* in this country.'

'A spy?'

'To put no finer point upon it, yes. Not an important operator in himself, but a link in a chain as we believe. You'll see the connection, of course—the connection with what your ship has been chartered for, Captain Halfhyde.'

'What was this man doing aboard my ship, do you know that?'

Wainscott said he could only theorize. Otto Leber had presumably been after information,

29

documents that might have been delivered to the Master of the *Taronga Park*, perhaps. His own information could have been faulty; he could have had his dates wrong and believed Halfhyde to be already aboard. He had, of course, been clumsy. His masters, who would not now admit any knowledge of him, would no doubt be displeased. But that, Wainscott said, was scarcely the point. It was obvious now that something had leaked and that the *Taronga Park* would be a marked ship.

'Then would it not be wiser to change your plans?' Halfhyde asked. 'Charter another ship—for whatever lies ahead?'

Wainscott shook his head. 'I have spoken on the telephone both to the Admiralty and the Foreign Office. The decision has been made to continue regardless.'

'Somewhat foolish, I would have thought.'

'That is not the official view. It's not one hundred per cent certain that the mission is jeopardized—Leber could have been working on some line of his own, without reference to those above him. On the other hand, if he was in fact following orders, which would pre-suppose a leak, then to call off the *Taronga Park* now would be tacitly to admit that we are on the track of—certain persons higher up the scale than Leber. To carry on might well disarm suspicion.'

'We act the innocents, Commander?'

'Yes, exactly. The German authorities will be unsure. That in itself may give us an advantage.'

'An advantage in the Amazon?'

'Yes.'

'I confess I don't see how. The diplomatic mind is a strange one.'

Wainscott laughed. 'I'd not disagree with that! But to return to my point that Leber may have been working on his own: we shall be seen as innocents in every respect. The identity of the dead man will not be mentioned. It will be reported in the press that it is a mystery and it will be allowed to fade from the news. In a very short time it will be entirely forgotten—'

'And the other man, the presumed watchman? Has my night-watchman, Platter, made an identification?'

Wainscott said he had; the second death was indeed that of the day-watchman, one Harry Laws.

'And will that, too, be conveniently forgotten?'

'Yes, of course. A common seaman, a person of no consequence,' Wainscott said, shrugging. 'There will be no fuss over that.'

'He may have a family. Has that been thought about?'

Wainscott shrugged again. 'If he has, then possibly a little money will change hands.'

Halfhyde sank back into the leather of the

cab seat. Just a common seaman, and some gold to buy off too many questions, plus threats very likely. It was a dirty business; it always was when the diplomats came into it. They were a different breed from the men of the sea, the simple sailormen who risked their lives daily against the elements and worse, and for starvation wages at that. The cab clattered on for the shipping office, where more men would sign away their freedom and perhaps their lives for more pittances, the scale laid down by the Board of Trade and one that with all the will in the world Halfhyde had not the money to increase. There was no more conversation: Wainscott had said all he was prepared to say and Halfhyde was left to wonder about what had been left unsaid. Time, of course, would tell him.

As the cab pulled up at the shipping office, outside which a milling crowd of seamen waited, Commander Wainscott broke his silence by saying, 'Your officers have already been chosen, Captain.'

Halfhyde flared at that. 'A damned liberty, Commander—'

'An essential one. You would have had to pick from among officers totally unknown to you. Those that await are good men, and trustworthy.'

'Perhaps so. I should have been informed of this at the Admiralty nevertheless.'

Wainscott shrugged again but didn't comment. He jumped down from the cab, followed by Halfhyde. They pushed their way past the waiting, hopeful men—some would be chosen, many left to take their chance when another shipmaster wanted a crew. It was like a cattle market, Halfhyde thought, human beings offering their bodies to those that would accept them and glad enough to sign aboard even a floating coffin.

Inside, they were ushered by a clerk to the Masters' room. Coffee was provided; they were joined by the shipping master before whom the crew would be signed. After an interval the shipping master left and the men who were to be Halfhyde's officers were shown in: first and second mates, chief and second engineers. Halfhyde's first impressions were mixed. The two deck officers appeared honest and tough, and, like himself, had done their time in sail. They carried recommends from previous masters, and in the case of the First Mate to be, a young man named Theophilus Briggs, the name of one of those masters was known to Halfhyde and respected. Halfhyde was not so sure about the two engineers, but was honest enough to admit to himself that in common with all seamen who had served in sail, and common with most naval officers as well, he had an instinctive dislike of the engine-room, which, with its oily smell and coal-dust, was bringing real sailoring to an end.

Halfhyde said crisply, after a word with each, 'Thank you, gentlemen. We shall meet again before the shipping master.'

When the officers had withdrawn Wainscott said, 'I think you'll find the Admiralty has chosen well enough, Captain.'

'Your own choice, do I take it?'

Wainscott nodded.

'You are a man of parts, Commander. Have you had experience yourself of merchant seamen and their abilities?'

'No, I have not. But I'm as well able as anyone else who knows the sea to assess a man's abilities—and to investigate backgrounds so as to assess that man's loyalties and dependability. You have good officers, Halfhyde. You may be assured of that.' Wainscott paused, then met Halfhyde's eye again with a gleam of humour in his own. 'If I'm wrong you may belabour me with blame. You see, I shall be sailing with you in the *Taronga Park*.'

Halfhyde's eyebrows went up. 'Will you indeed? I see. But not, I take it, as a commander in the Queen's service?'

'Yes and no,' Wainscott answered. 'That is, I shall not wear uniform except in certain circumstances, nor will the party that is to accompany me—'

'Party?'

'An armed party of seamen under a gunner's

34

mate.'

'For what purpose?'

'That you will be informed about later, Captain. For now there is simply the question of accommodation aboard. There will be some over-crowding I dare say ... and we must arrange for extra bunks to be fitted in your fo'c'sle mess.'

'Or hammock spaces. Naval ratings are more accustomed to hammocks, and they are easier to rig. And cheaper!'

'Well, perhaps.' Wainscott put a hand on Halfhyde's shoulder and went on, 'Never fear, the Admiralty pays. Remember you are being chartered. No expense will be spared.'

A minute or so later the shipping master returned to announce that the Articles of Agreement were ready for Halfhyde's signature. Two years' foreign-going, the agreement to be terminated automatically, as was usual, on the first return of the *Taronga Park* to a United Kingdom port. Halfhyde's crew would, by their signatures on the Articles, be committed perhaps to naval service if Wainscott's vague hints were borne out by events. To Halfhyde, there was a touch of the old-time press-gang about it, the grim, cruel days when men were taken off the streets by the press to be hustled to the dockyard hulks or straight to sea aboard the men-o'-war to fight the French, with not even the chance to take their leave of wives and parents and children.

CHAPTER THREE

The following days were busy ones: shore carpenters came aboard and extended the berthing arrangements in the fo'c'sle messroom. For Commander Wainscott there would be a spare cabin available in the engineers' accommodation beneath the poop, and the gunner's mate of the naval party would be accommodated with the bosun and carpenter, the two ship's petty officers, in the cupboard-like cabins on the side of the fo'c'sle opposite the deckhands. As soon as Halfhyde had returned from the shipping office, with his crew following on, the provisioning of the ship was started, with Halfhyde's steward, Barsett, making out the lists of requirements. Coal barges, towed by steam tugs, were laid on for the dirty business of taking bunkers for a long voyage; the *Taronga Park* would replenish her bunker at Funchal in Madeira and whilst on station supplies would be available at Georgetown at the mouth of the Demerara River in British Guiana.

Within a couple of hours of Halfhyde's return from the shipping office, Victoria had done wonders in the Master's accommodation. The cabin was free of its accumulated dust and was once again taking on the air of home. Halfhyde complimented her on it.

She was surprised. 'Well, thanks,' she said. 'What's come over you, mate, eh?'

He grinned down at her. 'Am I not always appreciative?'

'You're bloody not!' She put her hands on her hips and stared at him. 'I reckon I'm a fair home-maker, right?'

'Very right, my love.'

'Reckon I'd do a lot to a nice little house ashore.' She sounded wistful. 'Lace curtains, flowers in vases...'

'Aspidistra in the window.'

She nodded. 'Sure thing.'

'Just like Mrs Mavitty.'

She gave him a punch in the ribs. 'Only bloody thing I'm just like her, then. On second thoughts, no bloody aspidistra, mate! I'd like a garden, too. Not much, just enough space to grow some flowers.'

Despite what she had said the day before he saw the look in her eyes, a faraway vision of a permanent home, even the beginnings of a family. He shied away from it as always: he had no desire for the tied apron-strings, the constriction of the land; much as he had always loved his father's farm in Wensleydale, and the occasional company of dalesmen who had lived their whole lives in the one spot—he knew of farm labourers who lived in the tiny hamlet of Stalling Busk and who had never travelled farther than the market town of Hawes some four miles distant along the winding, narrow fell road—the land was not for such as he. He was wedded to the roll of a deck beneath his feet, to the challenge of calm and storm and of the fight against the sea, to the wondrous sunsets in the different parts of the world, to the star-studded arch of the sky at night with no building and no land configuration to obscure its totality, to the conversation of fellow seafarers with their tales from all the world's ports, the comradeship that always developed at sea at least until you attained command in either the Queen's ships or the merchantmen and became as one apart, aloof, God in his proper quarters...

Halfhyde left the cabin, walked along the narrow deck in front of the cabin ports. In the fore well-deck the derricks were busy, taking aboard cargo for Gurupá, which was to be cover only, but nevertheless was accompanied by proper bills of lading and had a genuine consignee: the British consul at the port of Santarem on the Tapajóz River, near its confluence with the Amazon. That cargo consisted of manufactured goods, a miscellany of articles not readily obtainable in Brazil whose manufactures were barely developed if at all. Halfhyde was cynical about that cargo: cover it might be, but the consul was no doubt looking to some feathering of his own nest.

The first mate, in overall charge of the loading operation so far as the stowage and the ship's trim was concerned, clearly knew his job and had a welcome air of authority about him as he moved from for'ard to aft where also the derricks were bringing cargo aboard. Halfhyde had already summed him up as a man who would take no nonsense from the fo'c'sle hands, who had proved to be as mixed a bunch as any that signed aboard a ship. Time would tell how handy they were in adverse weather: the best seamen still tended to sign aboard the windjammers where their skills could be put to the best use and where there was still pride in seamanship. Halfhyde, though he had a shrewd enough eye when picking a crew from the mob clamouring to offer their services, knew that he would be a lucky man if his choice proved not to have included a number of skrimshankers, sea lawyers and even men handy with a belaying pin for use on those with whom they fell out. Long voyages were never improvers of tempers. And much depended on the bosun, the man who stood between the officers of the afterguard and the rough-and-ready crowd in the fo'c'sle; but Halfhyde believed he had a good man. Bosun Taggart, solidly built and in his fifties, looked an honest, dependable fellow and had a valid reason for leaving the sailing ships in

39

which he had spent his life: a stiffened leg, the result of a fall from aloft some months previously, which precluded him from ever climbing out along a windjammer's yards again. He would find a steamer an easy option and Halfhyde had been glad to sign him on Articles.

ii

On the seventh day after the crew had been signed and the ship provisioned, the *Taronga Park* was in all respects ready for sea. The mud pilot, the river pilot and the tug had been ordered; the engines had been turned over for test a couple of days earlier and Mr Bannion, chief engineer, had reported all well in the engine-room.

The night before departure, the naval party—sixteen seamen plus a leading hand, under the gunner's mate, one Petty Officer Parker—had joined. They had come aboard singly or in twos, wearing plain clothes, and their rifles and side-arms had been delivered in wooden crates devoid of any government markings. They had been mustered out of sight in the fo'c'sle mess and PO Parker had come to report to Halfhyde and Commander Wainscott in the Master's cabin.

'Party all correct, sir.'

Wainscott nodded. 'Thank you, Parker. You've checked the rifles?'

'Yes, sir. Crates opened and examined and

then repacked.' The gunner's mate paused. 'Do the men work with the ship's crew, sir?'

Wainscott lifted an eye at Halfhyde and said, 'That's up to the Master. What do you say, Captain Halfhyde?'

'I say that idle hands do no one any good, least of all themselves.'

'I agree—'

'I shall be glad to have their services. There's still work to be done aboard. If your gunner's mate will liaise with my bosun, Commander, they'll work out a rota—with Mr Briggs' agreement.'

In the interest of maintaining secrecy until the *Taronga Park* had cleared away from Liverpool, no shore leave had been given on that last night in port. Word was not to reach the shore that naval personnel had been embarked, and there was none more talkative than a roistering, outward-bound crew drinking its last in a home port or going a-whoring as a farewell to England. There was a good deal of muttering amongst the crew but the bosun kept a firm hand on them and there was an extra watch on the gangway throughout the night, in which the naval men, still in their civilian clothes, took a part. And a little before midnight two more men came aboard from a private carriage that drew alongside with a rattle of harness. In the light of the flickering guard lantern they climbed the gangway and were

41

taken to the Master's cabin, where they were met by Halfhyde and Commander Wainscott, who made the introductions.

'Vice-Admiral Pelham-Grant ... and Mr Mayhew of the Diplomatic Service. Captain Halfhyde.'

Hands were shaken. Halfhyde turned a seaman's eye on the gentleman from the Foreign Office and found much wanting. Mr Mayhew was a sallow, jaundiced-looking man with lined cheeks and a black moustache; also with an air of obstinacy plus a touch of disdain as he stared around the cabin with eyes that looked in two directions at once, one ahead, the other with a left slant. This was, he seemed to be thinking, a far cry from the civilities of Whitehall. However, he said nothing out of place and the vice-admiral lost no time in coming to the point of his visit.

He reached into an inside pocket and brought out two sealed envelopes bearing the Admiralty's impress on the flaps. He handed one to Halfhyde, one to Wainscott.

'Your final orders, gentlemen. The envelopes are not to be opened until the ship is cleared from the Fastnet.' The vice-admiral paused, looking weightily at each in turn, then rose and fell on the balls of his feet. He was not a tall man; the action gave him greater impact. He went on, 'There will be dangers—you'll be aware of that, of course—'

Halfhyde broke in tartly. 'Yes, indeed I'm aware of that, sir, but only by inference. I have never been entrusted with any proper information. I am sailing blind, and into the unknown.'

Pelham-Grant nodded. 'Yes, quite. But you know enough, I think ... of matters that are not to be discussed here and now. The envelopes will provide much of the answer and I think your intelligence will tell you the rest ... and Mr Mayhew—though with discretion—will fill in the detail if required.'

Halfhyde stared. 'I see. Then I take it Mr Mayhew is to join my ship for—'

'For its destination, Captain. Yes, that is so.'

'I trust he'll enjoy the experience. The *Taronga Park* is no transatlantic liner, with all that that implies.'

'Quite so.' The vice-admiral, sensing the atmosphere, was placatory but obviously glad not to be sailing himself. 'However, I've no doubt you'll do your best to make him comfortable aboard your ship, Captain. I assure you his mission is a vitally important one and his presence aboard will be seen to be necessary if—er—if there is trouble at your destination.'

Trouble with the natives, Halfhyde thought, or trouble with the Germans? The rear-admiral in the Admiralty had spoken of the German Empire; and that empire was well-known to be heading along the dangerous path of expansion

43

and perhaps one day a clash of arms with the powerful old widow in Windsor Castle, grandmother of the German Emperor himself. The relationship would certainly not soften the approach of Kaiser Wilhelm, said not to be on good terms with the Queen-Empress, who was wont to over-ride him whenever they met. No doubt Mr Mayhew was there to use his Foreign Office charm—either that, or issue edicts in the name of Her Majesty's Secretary of State for Foreign Affairs, the noble Marquis of Salisbury. And the natives? Halfhyde gave an inward chuckle: the Brazilians, or anyway those around the Amazon River, might not be much impressed with diplomatic starch and Mr Mayhew would perhaps cut little ice with them. Probably the naval guard was there to cut the ice . . .

Mayhew and the sealed orders delivered, Vice-Admiral Pelham-Grant took his leave; and his carriage bore him away into the murk of the Liverpool night. Mayhew asked in some agitation where he was to be accommodated: currently that seemed to be his principal concern. Before Halfhyde could say that he would be provided with a cabin in the engineers' alleyway, Victoria Penn came in from the pantry.

Mayhew lifted shaggy eyebrows and flicked a silk handkerchief across his nostrils. Victoria said defiantly, 'Smell, do I?'

44

Halfhyde intervened. He introduced the diplomat and Victoria held out her hand, giving her urchin's grin. 'All right, mate,' she said, 'don't mind me, I'm just part of the bloody furniture, only I don't like blokes looking down their bloody noses at me, that's all.'

iii

The tug was alongside and Halfhyde was about to climb to the bridge next morning when Mr Mayhew chose a bad moment to state a complaint, the first of what Halfhyde guessed would be a lengthy list.

'Good morning, Captain—'

'Good morning, Mr Mayhew. I trust you slept well?'

'That's what I've come to see you about,' the diplomat said.

'But not now, if you please. I have to take my ship to sea.'

'Only a moment, Captain, and I insist.' Mayhew laid a hand on Halfhyde's arm, detainingly. Halfhyde looked down at it with displeasure. 'The cabin is small and far from comfortable, but I realize ships are not palaces. What troubles me is the noise from what I am told by the steward are steam pipes, an unpleasant gurgling—'

'Pipes will be pipes, Mr Mayhew.'

'And not only that.' Mayhew pursed his lips, sucking in his sallow cheeks and looking

45

disconcertingly in his two directions. 'There were drunken people about, singing and banging. There was drinking in the engineers' cabins, I believe. Is such conduct permitted aboard a ship, Captain?'

Halfhyde said, 'The night before sailing from the Mersey is an occasion, Mr Mayhew, and men denied shore leave are only human. Once we're at sea, there will be no drunkenness, I assure you.'

'And the gurgling, Captain?'

'That will continue. It is the way of steam pipes and water pipes. You'll grow accustomed to it.' Halfhyde turned away impatiently: the unberthing pilot was waiting for him already on the bridge. As he set foot on the ladder he saw Victoria's face behind the glass of one of the cabin ports. There was a grimace on it and a tongue was protruding towards the man from the Foreign Office. Halfhyde grinned but hoped Mayhew hadn't seen; he and Victoria Penn were going to be very unlikely shipmates. Ten minutes later, the *Taronga Park*, already singled up to the backspring, had her last rope slacked away, cast off and brought inboard and, in the care of the tug, was swinging for the lock that would take her into the main stream of the Mersey River to head out for the Skerries and away south down the Irish Sea. As his ship entered the river and turned for the open water Halfhyde watched the buildings of Liverpool

46

Town slide past, seeming in his fancy to bid their own farewell to yet another of Britain's ships starting out across the seas. Once again rain pocked the water. Commander Wainscott was on deck, in the after part of the ship, speaking to Petty Officer Parker, who, despite his civilian dress of blue jersey and canvas trousers beneath his oilskin, was standing rigidly at attention, back straight and head high: once a gunner's mate, Halfhyde thought, always a gunner's mate. They were a breed apart; along with the ships' corporals and the masters-at-arms who formed the ship's police aboard the men-o'-war, the gunner's mates were the mainstay of discipline and good order, descendants of the iron-hard men who had laid Lord Nelson's cannon on the enemy at Trafalgar.

Outside the river mouth, the pilot left the ship and the tug was cast off. The *Taronga Park* was on her own: Halfhyde began to feel the weight of responsibility brought by an unusual voyage. The dangers would not be purely human: the Amazon River, currently no more to him than the chart showed, was filled with navigational difficulties and it would not be easy to pick a way through the shoals that abounded in the channels. Also, the contiguous land would be forest and perhaps in places swampy, the river and tributaries no doubt filled with disease and possibly the haunt of alligators or crocodiles—and Halfhyde had an uneasy feeling that his duty was not going to confine him entirely to his ship.

Once the tug had been cast off and was steaming busily and smokily back into Liverpool, the voice-pipe from his cabin whined and he bent to answer it.

It was Victoria. 'Can I come up, mate?'

'It's raining,' he said.

'I know, but it's bloody stuffy down here.'

'All right.' He banged back the voice-pipe cover. Victoria came up, looking lost in Halfhyde's spare oilskin, her fair hair like a beacon atop the ungainly garment's black.

'That *bloke*,' she said.

'Mayhew?'

'Who bloody else? You know something, do you? Got a mouth like a chicken's arse, he has!'

Her voice was loud. He reproved her. 'We're not in Australia, Victoria. Ladies in England don't—'

'I've said before, mate, I'm no bloody lady. And what's wrong with bloody Australia, eh?'

He sighed. 'Bloody nothing,' he said. 'It's just that it's different, that's all.'

iv

The weather worsened as the *Taronga Park* steamed south through the Irish Sea for St George's Channel. The rain became a lashing downpour, driven into the faces of the bridge

48

watch-keepers by a blustery wind from the south-east. The ship rolled and pitched alarmingly, shipping water heavily over the fo'c'sle-head that then poured down over the tarpaulin-covered windlass to fling aft and thunder onto the covers of Number One hatch before continuing to swill around the base of the central island superstructure, turning it into an island. Halfhyde, remaining on the bridge while his ship fought the heavy, racing seas, held fast to a stanchion as the motion did its best to fling him bodily overboard. Victoria was down in the cabin now, taking shelter. The day wore on towards an early, bleak nightfall. There had been no sign of the man from Whitehall since the weather had worsened, but a report from the engineers' steward had indicated a corpse-like-figure inert and groaning on its bunk. The complaints would come later.

A little before eight p.m., Halfhyde began to note signs of an improvement: there was less weight in the wind and the seas were already tending to decrease. Less water was coming aboard although the motion of the ship was still more than restless, with the head dipping and then rising again in a series of stomach-wrenching jerks until once again she plunged bows under. But by midnight she was riding easier and the rain had stopped. The First Mate suggested that Halfhyde get some sleep. The worst, he said, was over.

'We're still in pilotage waters, Mr Briggs. There will be plenty of time for catching up on sleep once we've cleared the Fastnet.' Halfhyde paused. 'Also for picking your brains as to the Amazon River.' He had found that Briggs had made a voyage as an apprentice up the Amazon, at least as far as Pôrto de Mos at the point where the Xingú River met the Amazon itself. Commander Wainscott had indeed chosen well, though for all anyone aboard knew currently, the ship might be required to penetrate deeper into Brazil. Halfhyde was consumed with impatience, anxious for the Fastnet so that the seals on the Admiralty envelopes could be broken. The ship had been delayed by the weather that had forced a reduction in speed, but now that conditions had eased she was making progress. The Welsh coast slid past to port; and as dawn came up the summits of the Irish hills could be seen away to starboard.

By the time St David's Head had been raised on the port bow the day was bright and the wind had dropped right away; although the sea was still disturbed the ship was considerably more comfortable and from the bridge Halfhyde saw a shaky figure emerge from the engineers' alleyway and stagger with care for the starboard bulwarks.

He called down, 'A good night, I trust, Mr Mayhew!'

Mayhew waved a hand but made no other

response. He had a weakened, washed-out look even from a distance. Halfhyde turned away, scanning the shore through his telescope as they came down off St Bride's Bay between Ramsey and Skomer Islands. They continued south for the latitude of St Ann's Head outside the harbour of Milford Haven; and later as they came across the entry to the Bristol Channel a hail came down from the lookout at the foremast head: a small steamboat was coming out from Milford Haven and appeared to be closing the course of the *Taronga Park*. The First Mate—back on watch again after relief by the Second Mate from midnight to four a.m.—had already seen it and was watchful in case an alteration of course should become necessary.

Halfhyde laid his telescope on the boat. He said, 'It's a naval steam picquet-boat, Mr Briggs. A pound to a penny it's closing us for a purpose, though the Lord knows what.' More orders, further intelligence for Wainscott and Mayhew as to the Germans' intentions? A couple of minutes later a rating aboard the picquet-boat began sending a signal by semaphore: Halfhyde read it off. There was a passenger to be put aboard the *Taronga Park*. The mystery grew: who could the passenger be? Halfhyde was about to ask the person's identity when he saw a figure in the sternsheets of the picquet-boat rise to his feet and wave across the narrowing gap of water. A man in a blue serge suit, wearing a bowler hat which at that precise moment blew free from the head to be brought up short by the toggle secured to the man's lapel. It was Detective Inspector Todhunter from Scotland Yard.

v

Todhunter had been embarked by means of a Jacob's ladder sent down from the after well-deck by Bosun Taggart, who had personally leaned over the bulwarks and seized the shoulders of the ashen-faced detective inspector just in time to heave him inboard before his nerve gave way. Once Todhunter was aboard, a line was sent down and a heavy Gladstone bag was secured to its end and brought inboard. Todhunter gabbled a word of thanks and seized the bag's handle as though his life depended on the safety of its contents. Then he gave a start as he heard Halfhyde's shout from the bridge.

'What the devil does this mean, Mr Todhunter?'

Todhunter brought out a handkerchief and mopped at his face. 'All is well, Captain Halfhyde, I assure you.'

'Is it indeed! To the bridge at once, man, and explain.'

Todhunter shook his head in agitation and took a step along the deck towards the ladders leading upward. Halfhyde watched with interest, a smile lurking at the corners of his mouth: he recalled the policeman's dislike of ships and the sea during his previous voyage to South America, of his tendency to sea-sickness and a general unhandiness afloat. That had been aboard a battleship; Todhunter was not going to enjoy the discomforts of the much smaller *Taronga Park*.

Todhunter reached the bridge, breathing hard from his exertions. 'You seem surprised to see me, sir—'

'I am, Mr Todhunter. Is your sleuthing not confined to a search for our murderer back in Liverpool?'

Todhunter shook his head. 'No, it isn't. Frankly, I thought I had explained, when we met at the scene of the crime in the first instance. My involvement with that was no more than fortuitous, Captain Halfhyde. No more than fortuitous.' He hesitated, then came closer and lowered his voice. 'There is a need for secrecy. I'm afraid I can't say more. Just at present, you understand.'

'Not until the Fastnet?'

Todhunter looked puzzled. 'Pardon?'

Halfhyde said impatiently, 'Oh, never mind, it'll not be long. You'll have an hour or two to sling your hammock, then—'

'Hammock, Captain Halfhyde? Oh dear me, I'll never—'

53

'A figure of speech, Mr Todhunter, that's all, indicating you'll have time to settle down. If you're coming with us, you'll be given a bunk.'

Mr Todhunter was much relieved. 'My old mother,' he said conversationally, 'knew a sailor once. He was in his hammock when some unprincipled person cut the rope and—'

'An uncomfortable descent, Mr Todhunter, and one by no means unknown at sea. Have you breakfasted?'

It was an unkind question: the sea was being crossed by a swell, and the *Taronga Park* was rolling nastily. Breakfast would be out of the reckoning: the policemen's face was already green. Halfhyde suggested he made his way below to his, Halfhyde's, cabin. Barsett, Halfhyde's steward, would make arrangements for Todhunter's accommodation. Clutching his Gladstone bag, Todhunter went back down the ladder to the Master's deck and knocked at the cabin door. Victoria's voice bade him enter. He went in.

'Who're you?' she asked blankly, then remembered she'd seen him in Liverpool. 'Oh, it's you, mate! The peeler.'

'Detective Inspector Todhunter—'

'Same bloody thing.'

'From Scotland Yard.'

'Oh. You seen me mate, have you?'

'Your mate?'

She flipped a hand upwards towards the

bridge. Todhunter ticked over. It was, he thought, a very funny set-up; there were immoral overtones. He said stiffly, 'I've reported to Captain Halfhyde, yes.'

'Right,' she said. 'In that case you're bloody dinkum so you can bring your bloody arse to an anchor.'

Mr Todhunter's face had gone a deep red from embarrassment; he set what he had never ever thought of as his arse upon an upright chair and sat fiddling with his bowler hat and keeping a grip on the Gladstone bag. What a brazen woman! What his old mother would have thought was quite beyond imagining. Never in his life had Mr Todhunter heard his old mother, or his old father come to that, utter any expletive stronger than 'bother take it'. Of course, it had been different once he'd joined the Force, but the Force was a male preserve and even the cruder of his comrades never swore in the presence of the opposite sex. And his Chief Super was a stickler for the proprieties. Mr Todhunter wiped his face again with his handkerchief: he had started to sweat. What the woman would say next . . . and what she might do! He could become compromised if he wasn't very careful, very circumspect. Better to keep his trap shut and his knees together, with the Gladstone bag set like a blockhouse where she would fall over it if she came any closer and tried anything funny. His old mother had warned him about women: he was, she used to say, an attractive boy and would need to watch out.

On the bridge as the *Taronga Park* altered course to take her departure from below the Fastnet Rock, Halfhyde pondered the implications of the presence aboard his ship of a detective inspector of the Metropolitan Police.

CHAPTER FOUR

As the Fastnet was brought distantly abeam to starboard, Halfhyde lowered his telescope and spoke to his First Mate. 'Right, Mr Briggs. I shall be in my cabin if I'm wanted. But I'd prefer not to be disturbed unless it's necessary.'

'Aye, aye, sir.'

'Kindly send down to Commander Wainscott and Mr Mayhew. Tell them we're off the Fastnet now and that I await them.' Halfhyde went down the ladder, took a final look towards the distant shoreline, noted that the visibility was excellent and the weather apparently set fair, and went into his cabin to find Mr Todhunter hunched like a small animal at bay, with glazed eyes and a transfixed expression.

Victoria grinned and said, 'Hullo there, mate.' She moved across the cabin and her skirt swirled against Mr Todhunter, who seemed to become aware of Halfhyde for the first time. He scrambled to his feet, dodging the skirt.

'Beg pardon, Captain Halfhyde,' he said in a high voice.

'For what?'

There was a giggle from Victoria. 'For his dirty thoughts, I reckon,' she said.

Halfhyde frowned. 'That's enough, Victoria.'

'I never—'

'You heard what I said, Victoria. I must ask you to leave us—there is business to be discussed with Commander Wainscott and Mr Mayhew. And the day is bright and sunny—'

'All right, mate, I'm leaving.' Victoria gathered up her skirt and went to the door with a flounce. In the doorway she turned and stuck out her tongue at Halfhyde, who grinned back at her and made a shoo-ing motion with his hands.

'Well, I never did,' Mr Todhunter said, looking amazed. 'My Chief Super—' He stopped, blowing out his cheeks.

'Yes, Mr Todhunter?'

'It's not important, sir. Not important.'

'Good.' Halfhyde strode across the cabin and brought out a key on a chain around his waist. He unlocked his safe and extracted the two sealed envelopes from the Admiralty. The scuttle curtains swayed inwards with the ship's roll and Mr Todhunter averted his eyes and clasped his stomach. Then he reached into a

57

pocket and with hands that shook a little brought out a small bottle of pills. The legend on the label read 'DOCTOR DATCHET'S DEMULCENT DROPS'. Mr Todhunter shook out two tablets and consumed them.

Halfhyde asked, 'They still work satisfactorily?'

'You remember them, Captain Halfhyde? Yes, I expect them to be effective still. I should be lost without them, I do declare. My first use of them was aboard the paddle steamer that runs from the Clarence Pier at Southsea to Ryde in the Isle of Wight. A day trip, you know, with my old mother. Oh, years ago now. Years ago! How time passes, Captain Halfhyde.'

'Yes, indeed.' Halfhyde waved the envelopes at the detective inspector. 'These are about to be opened in accordance with Admiralty instructions. I take it you will wish to be present—that your presence is indeed connected with what may be in them?'

'That is correct, Captain Halfhyde, yes.'

'What, precisely, are you here for, Mr Todhunter?'

The answer was prompt. 'To represent the law of England, sir.'

'On the Amazon?'

'Yes, certainly.'

'H'm. I find that a strange proposition, Mr Todhunter.'

'Oh, by no means! Her Majesty's arm is a

long one, her—'

'It scarcely reaches to the Amazon, I think.'

Mr Todhunter had no immediate reply to that. He lifted a hand and scratched his face. 'Well, you'd be surprised,' he said.

'I am already. Have you a warrant to execute, Mr Todhunter?'

'Why, no, not exactly that, sir. Not exactly. Perhaps you could call it a watching brief.'

'I see. Do you know what is in these envelopes, by any chance?'

'Not except in the broadest sense, sir. But I think no more should be said until the other gentlemen are present. If I may be so bold, sir.'

Halfhyde nodded abstractedly, still in the dark as to the reason for Todhunter's presence. On that last occasion, years ago, the detective inspector had been armed with a warrant for the arrest of a traitor, Sir Russell Savory, late of the British Admiralty, fair enough game for the long arm of Her Majesty or whatever. But imagination boggled at the effect of a British policeman upon German nationals in Brazil, who were presumably carrying out, legitimately enough, their Kaiser's business. That was no concern of the Metropolitan Police but strictly that of the armed forces and of the Foreign Office . . .

Halfhyde was thinking this when there was a knock at his door and the representatives of both institutions entered the cabin, Commander

Wainscott briskly, for he was enjoying being back at sea from his desk in the Admiralty, and Mr Mayhew with a long-suffering, haunted look about him. His moustache was damp and limp with an unhealthy sweat and his face was as green as Todhunter's.

Halfhyde said, 'Good morning, gentlemen. The time has come ... you know Mr Todhunter, I believe?'

They nodded. Halfhyde handed one of the envelopes to Commander Wainscott. He said, 'Shall we open together?'

'Yes,' Wainscott said.

The man from the Foreign Office looked bored; he blew down his somewhat long nose, as if to indicate that he knew it all already. Halfhyde slit his envelope using an ivory paper-knife from his desk, then handed it to the commander. Each drew out a double sheet of Admiralty-crested writing paper.

Halfhyde read in growing exasperation; the *Taronga Park* was no steamroller, but he had the feeling his ship was being used to crack a nut. He said as much.

'Having said that, I would add that if there was real urgency, real threat, the Admiralty would have sent a stronger force than an unarmed ship—'

Mayhew broke in. 'The secrecy angle, Captain Halfhyde. Is it not obvious? A result in Her Majesty's favour is to be obtained not by *force* but by—'

'Subterfuge. Jiggery-pokery.'

'I dislike the phrase,' Mayhew snapped, a spot of colour coming to each side of the sallow, horse-like face. 'Her Majesty's Foreign Office does not indulge in jiggery-pokery.'

'I'll take your word for it,' Halfhyde said with a grin.

'Thank you. I'm much obliged. With your permission I shall summarize the content of the envelopes, leaving out the details and concentrating on the nub, the core of the wishes of HM Government and of my own chief, Her Majesty's Secretary of State for Foreign Affairs...'

Mayhew droned on for a while, establishing his own importance and his vital contribution to the mission; the actual summary failed to emerge and Halfhyde, becoming impatient, took over.

'I've already arrived at my own precis, Mr Mayhew. It is this: a despatch from our consul at Santarem advises that a German trading station is being set up on the Amazon, or rather on its tributary the Curuá River. This report appears to be verging on triviality—'

'Ah, but HM Government, as I was going on to say, Captain Halfhyde, believes there could be a deeper purpose, possibly hostile to Her Majesty's interests.'

'A guess? There seems to be no certainty

61

whatsoever.'

'Other than circumstantial,' Wainscott interrupted. 'It's well known that Kaiser Wilhelm has expansion of his empire much in mind. For a number of years now he's cast his eye towards South America. I think Mr Todhunter will bear me out?'

'Indeed yes, sir. Captain Halfhyde, too, will remember the traitor Savory in German pay! It's as plain as a pikestaff, sir.'

'Not to me,' Halfhyde said. 'Commander, what are your views?'

'On the German aspirations?' Wainscott frowned. 'As I said—expansion. More precisely, I suggest the Germans are hoping to establish a naval base from which our trade could be harried in the event of a war.'

'A naval base on the Amazon?' Halfhyde sounded derisive. 'Mud flats, sandbanks, all manner of hazards! River gunboats, perhaps—but such would scarcely be a major threat to our merchant shipping, I think, and still less to the fleet. Their range would be small enough.'

Wainscott shrugged. 'As I said, just a theory. We shall be finding out more. Indeed, to find out is our mission. We're not going in as a naval force to cut out the Germans.'

'We go in as spies?'

'An unfortunate word, Halfhyde. I prefer to say, we go in incognito.'

'As you wish,' Halfhyde said.

ii

Wainscott had remained in the cabin for further discussion with Halfhyde as to ways and means upon arrival and the safe navigation of the *Taronga Park* in the tricky waters of the Amazon. Todhunter and Mayhew left the cabin together, all but bumping into Victoria Penn, who had obviously been listening outside one of the scuttles. As they passed by, she dug Mayhew in the ribs and made some remarks which he failed to hear. He dodged backwards as though pricked by a pin and as they went down the ladder to the after well-deck the girl's laughter followed them.

Mr Mayhew was tight-lipped. 'An appalling woman, don't you agree?'

'Predatory sir.'

'Australian, I understand. She has no business to be on board, a *harlot* if ever there was one!'

'An apt word,' Mr Todhunter said with a prim pursing of his mouth.

'Ah?'

'Such was, in fact, her trade, sir, whilst resident in Sydney. Before being—er—acquired by Captain Halfhyde, I should hasten to add.' Todhunter revealed the result of enquiries made of the Admiralty by his Chief Super.

'Goodness gracious me!'

Todhunter shrugged. 'The desires of seafarers, sir—'

'Yes, yes. A low lot to be sure. Women and drink are their main preoccupations. However, it never occurred to me that I should ever have to endure the company of a—a strumpet.'

'Quite so, sir.' Mr Todhunter, a far from inexperienced policeman, stole a sideways glance at the diplomat. Something about Mr Mayhew told him very distinctly that, like seafarers, strong desires lurked but were in Mayhew's case kept well hidden beneath the surface, behind his sweaty and unprepossessing looks. Sweat, now: a manifestation of lewd thoughts? But his clamminess could, of course, be due to sea-sickness: in that, Mr Todhunter had a fellow feeling. When the *Taronga Park* gave a more than usually vicious pitch and roll, the diplomat moved for the guardrail and Todhunter found his diagnosis correct. He uttered a timely word of warning, one given him during his sojourn aboard the battleship in his pursuit of the traitor Savory.

'The other side, sir, if I may make so bold.'

'Why?'

'Because on this side, sir, the wind is blowing straight into your face.' Mr Todhunter reached into his pocket, then brought his hand away empty. It was in his nature to be a good samaritan but the voyage might well prove longer than expected and Dr Datchet's

Demulcent Drops, which soothed and protected the stomach and directed its contents down rather than up, wouldn't last for ever.

iii

Commander Wainscott, in Halfhyde's view, was over confident. He seemed to be placing too much reliance on his gunner's mate and the armed seamen, who would be landed as required and used as a background threat if the Germans should prove recalcitrant, recalcitrance being interpreted as opposition to the wishes of the British Government that they should depart bag-and-baggage.

'Unlikely,' Halfhyde said, with more than a touch of impatience. 'They will have their orders.'

'Obviously, yes—'

'And we're not to use force. We haven't any force in any case, apart from your seamen.'

'The orders refer to the *threat* of force, Halfhyde. That we can use, and will use if necessary—'

'You mean a despatch to the Admiralty, asking for warships to be sent?'

Wainscott nodded. 'Yes. That's provided for.'

'A despatch will take weeks!'

'Possibly, since there's no cable station at Santarem and the route is roundabout—but bear in mind the orders, Halfhyde: to send for

65

warships is to be a last resort. Our mission is peaceful, and must take the form of persuasion in the first instance.'

'Parading the guard ostensibly for ceremonial purposes only ... and pleading family loyalties as opposed to patriotic ones?'

Wainscott frowned and blew out his cheeks. 'Scarcely that. The Kaiser, as we know, disdains such feelings and is impatient with his grandmother who treats him as a little boy—which is why he seldom stays at Windsor Castle or the palace. Also, he regards his uncle the Prince of Wales as an absurd figure, a man more interested in amusing himself than in affairs of state and empire. No, we shall not gain our objective along such lines as family loyalties, Halfhyde.'

'Quite. My suggestion was frivolous. But how *do* we gain these objectives, Commander?'

Wainscott indicated the written orders. 'It's all there, Halfhyde.'

'No, sir, it is not!' Halfhyde took up the sheet and waved it at the naval officer. 'This is the customary rubbish from Whitehall, so constructed that anything we do can be used against us if Their Lordships so wish it—worded in such a way that there is always a let-out for the powers that be, who can disown us at the drop of a hat. There is nothing precisely stated, merely hinted at by way of suggestion. The decisions are left to us—you

66

and Mayhew and in a navigational sense myself, and woe betide any of us if we put a foot wrong! Though I dare say Mr Mayhew has covered himself well enough and will slip out of any trouble like a snake leaving its hole. I—'

'Really, my dear Halfhyde, there's no—'

Halfhyde flung the sheet down on his desk and thumped it with his fist. 'The orders, sir, are simple bullshit!'

Wainscott flushed and got to his feet. 'Then there is no point in our continuing to discuss them,' he said, and marched out of the cabin.

Halfhyde swore to himself: once again his temper had got the better of him. He was up against his old enemy: Admiralty wiliness, the ever-present tendency of Their Lordships and their political masters to leave the greatest possible number of loopholes that could cause the eventual strangulation of officers on the spot at sea. On this occasion he saw himself as very much the sacrificial lamb: there could be no more fraught a situation than one in which the world's mightiest monarchs were at each other's throats in the matter of building up empires. It was by no means impossible that the orders had been initiated by Her Majesty in person; uppity grandsons had to be given their come-uppance, perhaps, and he, Halfhyde, was to be part of the weapon to be employed in satisfying the ego of an imperious old lady safe behind her guards at Windsor Castle and Buckingham Palace.

Halfhyde was staring from the port, seeing little but an oval face, a mouth turned down at the corners, and a bun of hair beneath a widow's cap, when Victoria came into the cabin.

'Well, mate.'

He swung round, glaring, the vision still before his eyes.

She looked back at him. 'What's up, eh? You've got a kind of mad look, mate.'

'I dislike this business,' he said. 'I—'

'You didn't have to bloody take it on,' she said, reasonably enough. 'Money's not everything, is it, eh?'

'It is,' he snapped, 'when you haven't got any and you have a ship to pay for, and a crew to feed.'

She giggled. 'And me.'

'Yes. And you.'

She gave her head a shake, looking puzzled. 'There's more than that got into you, mate. Let's have it, eh?'

He took a deep breath. 'I simply wish the Queen had been less inclined to give way to Prince Albert's will when he was alive. I wish she hadn't given birth to so many females who married Europe's crowned heads and brought the entire continent under her sway, beneath her damned interfering will! It's a sorry state of affairs when the world's peace can hang upon the private dislikes between the German Empire

68

and its confounded grandmother!'

Victoria was still bewildered. 'Don't know what you're bloody talking about, but it sounds disloyal to me, mate. We go a lot on the Queen, down under, and I reckon—'

'I'm far from disloyal and I shall do my duty. And you, Victoria, will not repeat anything I've said. Is that understood?'

'An order, eh?'

'Yes. There's secrecy around still—in the national interest. To talk would be an act of treason.'

She jeered. 'Go on, lay it on thick like treacle, eh? Any talk, and the Queen, she can bloody hang us, right?'

iv

The weather continued fair, the days passing with no more than a gentle breeze, as the *Taronga Park* headed on a southerly track for Madeira. As they dropped south the air became balmy though overlaid with the reek of black smoke from the furnaces. Out at sea, there was no reason to hide the naval party; and soon enough the ship's crew would know what they were there for. Thus Petty Officer Parker requested permission for them to muster in their uniforms for arms drill on the fore well-deck. This permission given, they turned out smartly in white duck blouses and bell-bottoms, gaitered and belted and carrying

69

their rifles and bayonets, to be fallen in and marched up and down the restricted space to the loud shouts of command from the gunner's mate.

Halfhyde watched from the bridge: the scene and the shouts brought back past days when he had sailed in the Queen's ships from midshipman to lieutenant. Days of calm and storm, of autocratic admirals and captains, largely gin filled and choleric in their dealings with junior officers, remote from the common seamen to whom they seldom addressed a remark other than at the defaulters' table, days of seamen doubling round the upper deck for exercise . . .

Petty Officer Parker, knowing that many eyes were upon him, shouted with a will, drilling his seamen for a full two-hour stretch as the *Taronga Park* lifted and plunged to the long swell of the North Atlantic into which they had now passed. At the end of the two hours the men were wet with sweat and their feet, in heavy ammunition boots, were sore.

Petty Officer Parker fell them out. 'Right, my lucky lads! That'll do for now. Turn for'ard . . . dis-*miss*!' There was a clatter and a clank of rifles and bayonets as the guard obeyed the order and moved thankfully for the peace and calm of the fo'c'sle. The gunner's mate, falling himself out as well, put a quid of tobacco into his mouth and started chewing: his teeth showed the dark brown result of a good deal of past chewing, a stain not unlike that of an Indian or Malayan native who had spent a lifetime chewing betel nut. Making his way aft to report to Commander Wainscott, Parker chanced upon Victoria Penn sunning herself on the hatch over in the after well-deck. He halted.

'You want to watch the sun, miss.' He looked lasciviously at the bare flesh of arm and leg, with some thigh visible. 'Does funny things.'

She laughed. 'Me, I'm used to it, mate.'

Mate! Parker liked that; the captain's piece addressing him as mate must certainly indicate friendliness and currently Halfhyde was not in view. He said, 'I 'eard you come from Australia.'

'Dead right I do. You been there, have you?'

Parker shook his head. 'Never. I done my service China-side an' up the straits,' he said, the latter reference being to Gibraltar and the Mediterranean station. 'That's apart from Pompey.'

'Pompey?'

'Portsmouth. Guz is Devonport.' Petty Officer Parker had moved closer and was still chewing. The smell of tobacco was strong and a little juice was running from the corner of his mouth. 'There's a lot I can tell you about the navy, miss. That's if you're interested.' He gave a leer: he couldn't achieve much on deck apart from lay the foundations, but once that had

71

been done a more propitious moment might come. The girl didn't look the sort for a bloke like that Captain Halfhyde, who by all accounts had not so long ago been a lieutenant in the Queen's ships and looked a right stuck-up one at that. The girl was of Parker's own class, more accustomed to the lower deck than the wardroom—that stuck out a mile every time she opened her mouth. Parker edged a little closer, then sat down on the hatch cover and allowed his hand to touch against bare flesh. It felt good.

Victoria asked, 'Interested in what, eh?'

'Like I said. The navy.'

'Like fuck,' Victoria said distinctly. Petty Officer Parker gave a start. That wasn't the way women talked, except maybe in Queen Street, Pompey, close to the barrack hulks in the dockyard, and that was different. The Australian bit's intonation had held no hint of anything like an invitation. 'I'm not grass green, mate, I come from Sydney. Know something?'

'Know what?' Parker mumbled.

'You come half a bloody inch closer with your bloody sweat and tobacco juice and I'll shove a hatpin where it bloody does most damage.'

72

The *Taronga Park* entered the port of Funchal in Madeira, overshadowed by the steep sides of Pico Ruivo which rose to more than six thousand feet. Halfhyde brought the ship to an anchorage and a signal was made by flags asking for bunkers. After some delay a Portuguese official from the shipping agents came out in a small steamboat to collect payment in advance, and some while after this a string of lighters was seen approaching under tow of a steam tug. Once alongside, it was a case of all hands to the dirty business of bunkering from the coal-filled lighters. Soon the ship was covered above and below with a thick layer of coal-dust. Halfhyde, though well used to the evolution of coaling a man-o'-war, looked at it all with distaste, thinking of the cleanliness of sail and the free supply of the world's great winds; coal cost a good deal of money. So did provisions, which came out in another boat after the coaling was complete and Mr Bannion, chief engineer, had reported his bunkers full to capacity.

The provisions aboard and no shore leave given, the *Taronga Park* weighed her anchor and proceeded on passage for the Amazon River. Mr Todhunter shook coal-dust from his bowler hat and with regret watched the shore-line recede behind as the ship headed out on her westerly course. There would be no more land now until the Brazilian coast loomed

73

with all its dangers, so very different from the streets of London where the only threats were footpads and pick-pockets and such, with an occasional murder thrown in. Mr Todhunter mopped at his face with his handkerchief: it came away black. He clicked his tongue; the sea was an unpleasant place. He must go below for a wash, if there was enough water—but of course there would be. Seawater only though; fresh was for drinking. Mr Todhunter much disliked washing in salt water, which left a stickiness behind. He gave a sigh, a heartfelt one. What, really, was a detective inspector doing aboard a ship bound on a clandestine mission to prevent the German Navy establishing a base overseas? He could scarcely arrest them and charge them—Captain Halfhyde had made that very point indeed—and tell them that what they said would be written down and might be given in evidence. He would be a laughing stock. On the other hand his Chief Super was no fool; he would know what he was doing. A purpose must lurk somewhere and would manifest itself at the proper time. And whatever it was, if he, Todhunter, could bring it to a successful conclusion, then a long delayed promotion must surely lie upon the cards when he returned to the Yard. He would put his best foot foremost when he knew whereabouts it was required to be put. His career was precious; it had filled his

74

life since the passing away of his old mother, to whom he had been devoted. Often on what he thought of as stilly nights Mr Todhunter had looked upwards to the stars and thought of her somewhere behind and above, enjoying her eternal rest but at the same time keeping a motherly eye on him in his mortal coil below. And really, it *was* a coil at times! There was no denying that. His Chief Super, and no disrespect intended, could be a hard and tiresome man. There had been times since sailing from Liverpool, and this was one of them, when Mr Todhunter had come to suspect that he was afloat principally because his Chief Super wanted him out of the way...

That was a sad reflection on human nature and Mr Todhunter told himself sternly that it was mere fantasy. Then he went below to wash away the coal-dust. As he entered the engineers' alleyway he saw Mr Mayhew look out from his cabin, the sallow face peering from over a starched white stand-up collar now limp from the close heat.

Todhunter said, 'Good afternoon, sir.'

'Ah, Todhunter.' The Foreign Office man drew his door curtain fully aside and stood revealed in his shirt, the cuffs of which were as limp as the collar. 'A word with you, if you please.'

There was something conspiratorial about the diplomat. Mr Todhunter, much intrigued, said,

'By all means, Mr Mayhew, sir. By all means.'

CHAPTER FIVE

'You would care for a drink, perhaps? I have whisky.'

'No, thank you, sir. I'm a teetotaller.'

'Ah.' Mayhew poured himself a stiff three fingers, very little water.

'I've signed the Pledge, sir.'

'Yes, I see. Very wise, I've no doubt. Policemen have to be careful, of course.'

'Yes indeed, sir, very careful.'

'So have we in the diplomatic.' Mayhew sipped. 'I do not refer specifically to alcohol, you understand.'

'Quite, sir, yes.' Mr Todhunter fidgeted, sitting on an upright chair with his back against Mayhew's wash-hand stand, a tall structure of mahogany with a flap that let down to produce a basin, with beneath it a can to catch the used water when the basin was tipped. Mr Todhunter felt ill at ease with Mayhew. There was, of course, a point somewhere but the diplomat was taking a longish while to get to it. Was he, perhaps, about to reveal more about their mission—reveal, perhaps, what it was that he, Detective Inspector Todhunter, was expected to do? When Mayhew frowned and

76

pulled at his long chin but said nothing further, Mr Todhunter took his courage in both hands and put a question himself.

'Beg pardon, sir . . .'

'Yes?'

Todhunter coughed. 'If I may make so bold, sir. My own orders are, well, to put no finer point upon it, sir, imprecise.'

'What are they, Todhunter?'

'To embark, sir, and be handy by.'

Mayhew raised an eyebrow. 'Was that all?'

'Yes, sir. To represent the law if needs be.'

'Imprecise indeed! Frankly, I see no use for you at all.'

Mr Todhunter flinched a little: that was very near the bone. He said uncomfortably, 'Well, sir, that seems to dispose of the question I was going to put, with respect.'

'You were about to ask?'

'If you could tell me what I'm here for, sir.'

'As to that, I know no more than you. But I would suggest that it's possible the Admiralty has some information that it has not seen fit to pass to me. Such as the possibility that British nationals could be involved with the Germans upon the Amazon—'

'Dear me, sir, yes, that *is* a possibility!' Todhunter wiped sweat from his face: the small cabin was close and held the smell of whisky, which was rather sick-making. 'If that should be so, then I might be required—'

'Exactly. And I am wondering if you have any information on that score? I understand it was by Admiralty request that you were seconded to the *Taronga Park*, Todhunter.'

'Why yes, sir, that is certainly so. But I'm afraid I have no knowledge of—er—of—'

'Clandestine orders?'

'Clandestine, sir? I—'

'Orders that by some oversight were not made known to me.'

'Oh no, sir, no indeed! A gentleman from the Foreign Office ...' Todhunter flushed with embarrassment, having by this time arrived at the reason for his being lured into Mayhew's cabin: Mayhew was seeking information for himself. In a way it was very flattering, of course; Mr Todhunter's embarrassment was largely due to his being unable to assist the quality, no one being more entitled than the Foreign Office gentleman to be classed as quality. It was at the same time humbling for a mere detective inspector to be asked for help by a diplomat, a person pretty close to Her Majesty the Queen. It was also a bit odd, really. If Mr Mayhew didn't know what was going on, then who did?

'I'm really very sorry, sir,' Todhunter said, and made to rise to his feet. He was stopped: Mayhew raised a hand and Todhunter dropped back onto the chair, striking the wash-hand stand hard with his rump so that the can beneath rang like a gong.

'A word upon another matter, Todhunter.'

'Yes, sir.'

'The woman Penn. You already know my personal views, of course.'

'Yes, indeed I do, sir.'

'Those views were, I stress, personal. But I believe there is another angle.'

'You do, sir?' Todhunter asked uncertainly.

Mayhew seemed to stretch his lips, and in so doing showed a line of yellowed teeth, others black and broken. Todhunter stared as if mesmerized: Mr Mayhew had quite a devilish look, made worse by his squint. The teeth vanished when the diplomat went on, 'I refer to the question of ... I was going to say loyalties, but possibly it is too strong to suggest that the woman has the brain, the *intellect* required to be any threat in that particular direction. Yet I see dangers, Todhunter. The very fact of her presence could threaten our success, albeit unwittingly. But to represent this to Captain Halfhyde is the sheerest waste of time and breath. He is besotted.'

'Or loyal, sir.'

'Loyal?' Mayhew's eyebrows went up. 'To a strumpet, Todhunter?'

'I'm sorry, sir.'

'The woman should never have been allowed to remain aboard. However, she is here. I'm asking you to keep an eye on her, as closely as possible.'

'She can't go far away, sir. Not at sea.'

'I realize that, Todhunter. But once we reach the Amazon, and the land, then it might be a different story.'

'In what way, sir, if I may ask? What do you see her doing?'

Mayhew pursed his lips. 'Who knows? Women are women, Todhunter, and—'

'Well, yes, that's right, sir. Very right. Oh, dearie me, sir!' Todhunter almost slapped his thigh. 'I've had dealings with women before now, and I do agree, there's just no knowing. No knowing at all. My Chief Super, he always made a point of stressing—'

'Yes, yes, Todhunter. I'm sure you have the intelligence to know what I mean. A woman among many men is always a potential hazard.'

'You mean doubtful moral business, sir? If I may put it that way.'

Mayhew nodded. 'There's always the chance, of course. How climate affects women is well enough known. Men, too, I suspect. Yes, trouble could come from the mere fact of her—er—womanhood. Jealousies—you understand, of course.'

'Of course, sir.' In a way Todhunter did understand, though not from any experience of his own. Romance had tended to pass him by, though once—when he'd been a mere uniformed constable belamped and bewhistled on the beat around Leicester Square and had assisted to her feet a literally fallen woman, a slip of a girl in fact, lying in the mud and in danger from the passing hooves of carriage horses—on that occasion a shaft of naked passion had pierced his heart. Or perhaps, looking back, it had been just sympathy. In any case, the stench of drink had been strong and Constable Todhunter's Salvation Army principles had come to his aid and he'd blown his whistle for another constable to help him drag the girl to the police station. Once there, she had been loudly vituperative, calling Todhunter a bastard, and the remnants of passion had died. But yes, he did understand aroused feelings. If women were women, men were men. He had been proud of his arousal. It had not occurred since.

'I think you should watch for that too, Todhunter?'

'Watch for—' Todhunter's mind was still in the past. 'Oh yes, sir. But with respect, surely Captain Halfhyde—'

'Captain Halfhyde has his ship to attend to, Todhunter, and in moments of navigational stress can't be everywhere at once. The woman could take advantage.'

'Oh, I don't think so, sir. From what I've seen, she's devoted—'

'Yes, no doubt. I'll put it another way: *others* might take advantage of the captain's preoccupation. And you are the one man I can approach, the only man of rank aboard apart from myself and Commander Wainscott who is independent of the ship's crew. Also you are a policeman, Todhunter, a man of integrity and authority. I call upon you to exercise your office. I trust I shall not call in vain.'

A pompous gentleman, Todhunter thought to himself. He said, 'Indeed not, sir. Indeed not.'

Leaving Mayhew's cabin Todhunter shook his head in some bewilderment. Of course, Captain Halfhyde's woman could cause the kind of trouble Mayhew had in mind but Todhunter could see no way in which her conduct could affect the success of the mission, unless Mayhew believed she might be approached by the Germans and in some way made use of. But Todhunter thought that most unlikely: she surely wouldn't allow herself to be suborned by the Queen's enemies and there was no doubt of her devotion to Captain Halfhyde. Indeed, Todhunter himself had found he could not help but have a degree of sneaking liking for her however appalling her morals and forwardness—it was a pity about the moral situation, which posed quite a dilemma to a God-fearing man. Suddenly he recalled his earlier meeting with Mr Mayhew and his suspicion that the diplomat was hiding lascivious thoughts. Could it be not entirely impossible that he, Todhunter, was being used by Mr Mayhew as a kind of self-protection? If there was a detective inspector always on the watch for doubtful moral business, it would be that much easier for Mayhew to control his desires which otherwise might get the better of him. For a diplomat, that would never do.

Well, well.

ii

Commander Wainscott busied himself in the chart room, in company with Halfhyde scanning the shallows and mud flats of the Amazon with its seaward approaches and many tributaries. It was quite an astonishing area: its basin, together with that of the Tocantins, covered no less than two and three-quarter million square miles; or, put another way, two-fifths of the entire South American continent. Flowing on average three miles an hour, the river discharged nearly two and a half million cubic feet into the Atlantic per second, together with large quantities of solid matter—dead monkeys, pumas, sloths, armadillos, snakes and the occasional Brazilian, plus wood debris from the native dwellings often shattered by the waters in times of flood. Flood was one of the hazards, for during high water periods the level rose some twenty-six feet to a depth of sixty feet, all in something of a rush; while at spring tide there was a formidable bore as far as four hundred miles up stream.

'We shall have our work cut out,' Wainscott said. 'It's easy to see why the Admiralty didn't charter a larger ship.'

Halfhyde shrugged. 'I shall cope, with Briggs' assistance.' He rubbed at his long chin as bright sunlight struck through the port, glinting on polished brass fittings. He went on reflectively, 'I've been thinking about our consul at Santarem, who has stirred all this up. You said you'd met him, Commander. I fancied you were non-committal.'

'Possibly . . .'

'Is there something I should know?'

Wainscott said, 'Oh, I don't think so. Millington's not a bad chap as consuls go.'

'Santarem's a backwater, Commander.' Halfhyde paused. 'Should I take it that the man is fitted to the job?'

Wainscott laughed. 'I'm bound to say you could take it that way, yes. The climate, you know—it doesn't help.'

'Drink?'

'He takes his noggin. He's no dynamo. Lets his dress and standards go from time to time. But he's conscientious mostly, and loyal.'

'Good. Tell me, Commander—have you met him since his appointment to Santarem?'

Wainscott said he hadn't; he'd known Millington a few years previously, when he'd been a consular agent in Japan. The drink, he said, had been something of a problem, going beyond the usual round of entertaining and being entertained.

'And Santarem . . . not quite Japan. Different drinking. Little social life in Santarem, I would guess. Solitary drinking seldom produces efficiency in my view.'

Wainscott said with a touch of irritation, 'He happens to be all we've got once we enter the Amazon, Halfhyde. We must make the best of him.'

Halfhyde, staring broodingly from the port, didn't respond. A possible alcoholic and seedy consul to represent British interests would be no great help, and their mission was in any case somewhat nebulous, every move they made liable to be misconstrued by the Admiralty. Leaving Wainscott poring over the charts, Halfhyde moved out to the bridge, where the Second Mate was on watch. He looked down at his decks fore and aft: they were spotless. Taggart had proved a good bosun, keeping everything shipshape despite the filthy engine fumes that were currently blowing over the bridge from the tall, thin funnel set just aft in the engine-room casing, blown along a light breeze from astern, a wind that was just a fraction faster than the ship's own speed. As Halfhyde looked for'ard Petty Officer Parker moved along the deck to rouse out the naval party and once again weary them with his drill.

Parker vanished into the fo'c'sle. Idly, Halfhyde after a while registered that the gunner's mate had been gone for some time. Soon after this he reappeared together with two hands of the naval party; there seemed to be some kind of altercation in progress, and Parker kept glancing up at the bridge.

Halfhyde called down, 'Petty Officer Parker.'

'Yessir!' Parker came to attention and saluted.

'You have a worried look.'

'I reckon I have at that, sir. There's a compartment I'd like opened up, sir, beneath the fo'c'sle mess—'

'Which compartment, and why do you wish to open it up?'

Parker said, 'I reckon it's the cable locker, sir—'

'Cable locker? What's wrong with it? I'd sooner not have it opened up at sea—you know the dangers of heavy links that might move with the ship's motion.'

'Aye, sir, I do. But the men, sir—they've complained of a stench coming from below and I reckon it must be from the cable locker, sir.'

'Have you spoken to the bosun?'

'Aye, sir, and he reckons it's dead rats, nothing to worry about he says, but I don't know so much—'

'When did the complaints start, Parker?'

'Only just this morning, sir.' Parker paused. 'I reckon something's beginning to notice the heat, sir. More'n rats, sir. More like it's a 'uman body.'

CHAPTER SIX

'There's something of a stench, certainly.' Halfhyde, going himself to the cable locker, recognized the smell of death, unmistakably. With Halfhyde were Taggart, two able seamen of the ship's crew, Petty Officer Parker and Detective Inspector Todhunter, the latter attending in his official role and bustling with an air of importance.

'This may have a connection with Liverpool, Captain Halfhyde, sir.'

'Possibly.' It was, Halfhyde thought, a longish time since Liverpool and the first discovery of bodies. True, the conditions in the port had been cold enough; but surely decomposition would have set in long before now? 'If there is a body I doubt we shall ever know an identity, unless it carries papers.'

'Why so, sir?'

'The cable has been worked since then, that's why. And the links are heavy.'

Todhunter nodded, using his imagination. The mangling effect of heavy steel cable, the links flinging about as the anchor was let go with a run, fragmented flesh ... he gave a shudder. How terrible, if perhaps the man had been alive to start with! He watched in silence as the two able seamen removed the big plate covering the hatch that gave access, in port, to the cable locker via the upper part of the navel pipe. The *Taronga Park* was rolling in the ocean swell and dull clanks could be heard as the cable shifted in the navel pipe. Todhunter glanced at the bosun, who was holding a lantern above his head to light the enclosed, airless place beneath the fo'c'sle. Taggart was looking sick, as sick as Todhunter himself was feeling. The smell, as the hatch was opened up, became much worse. Todhunter retched, then steeled himself: he was a policeman, after all. This was part of his job.

Halfhyde pushed past, put his head through the hatch, carefully. In the light from the lantern Todhunter could see the swinging cable as it led up to the drum of the windlass on the deck above.

'Lantern,' Halfhyde said in a muffled voice. Taggart moved forward and handed the lantern over. It shone down into the murky depths, casting shadows. Halfhyde peered down for a full minute, then withdrew his head, his face greenish in the lantern's light.

'I can see nothing,' he said. 'But that there's something there is plain enough. Taggart?'

'Aye, sir?'

'We'll go up on deck. Leave the hatch open.' Halfhyde turned away and went up the ladder to the deck, followed by the others. The sun was hot, though the following wind brought some freshness. They all took deep breaths. Halfhyde called up to the bridge, addressing the Second Mate.

'Mr Harrison, I intend to veer cable. The engine to stop, and be good enough to rouse out Mr Briggs. My compliments, and I'd like to see him at the windlass.'

'Aye, aye, sir.'

The bell of the engine-room telegraph rang on the bridge and was repeated from below. The engine died, the thump of the machinery ceased, the shaft lay idle. There was a curious silence broken only by the sigh of the wind through the rigging. As the *Taronga Park* lost her motion through the water and rolled sluggishly, the First Mate came aft along the well-deck to report to Halfhyde.

'You sent for me, sir?'

'Yes, Mr Briggs. I propose to veer cable.'

Briggs was surprised. 'At sea, sir?'

'Yes.' Briefly Halfhyde explained. By this time the ship's carpenter was standing by the windlass. Briggs had a word with him, then climbed the ladder to the fo'c'sle-head along with the bosun and some hands who began unsecuring the anchor from the cathead. When

89

the anchor had been lowered on its strops to hang from the hawse-pipe on the shackle at the end of the cable, Halfhyde gave the order to veer on the windlass. Steam hissed and slowly, very slowly, the cable was paid out, the anchor vanishing beneath the surface.

Halfhyde said, 'I shall veer all the way to the Senhouse slip.' He turned to Todhunter. 'You and I shall go below again, Mr Todhunter.'

ii

It took a long time; the Senhouse slip, Todhunter discovered, was right at the very bottom of the cable locker, secured to the great ring-bolt that was the final holding place of the cable's inboard end. There was an unconscionable amount of cable, Todhunter thought as he held his handkerchief tight to his nostrils. And it was going out so slowly. Halfhyde had explained that slowness was vital: with the anchor dangling about in deep water an immense strain had come upon the cable and undue stress was to be avoided at all costs.

As the cable went past the open hatch Halfhyde examined each link in the light from the lantern. By his side stood one of the seamen holding a wash-deck broom. Todhunter watched as from time to time segments of flesh, vile and decomposed, were brushed off to drop to the bottom of the locker. There was now no possible doubt about the presence of a human

90

body: already a severed leg, caught by the links of the cable, had appeared briefly and had been dislodged by the broom. There was a thud as it hit the locker bottom. Todhunter's flesh crawled: Captain Halfhyde seemed to have nerves of steel.

At last the cable tightened and Halfhyde roared out the order to belay. With the cable now up-and-down from the Senhouse slip, the racket of the windlass above ceased. Once again there was silence.

Halfhyde said, 'Now we go down.'

'Down?'

'Into the locker. There's footholds cut out of the bulkhead. I'll go first.'

Todhunter swallowed hard. He could scarcely refuse; to do so would be not only cowardly but unpolicemanlike. Duty was his watchword. In something close to sheer terror he watched Halfhyde, still carrying the lantern, swing a leg over the hatch coaming and begin his descent.

Halfhyde's voice came up hollowly: 'Now, Mr Todhunter. Take it carefully. Feel for your footholds and handholds.'

Todhunter gave something like a bleat. Shaking but once again steeled, he gripped the hatch coaming tightly and swung a leg over as Halfhyde had done. He reached around with it until his boot rested on something firm upon which he could perhaps put his weight. He did so, gingerly; it held. Lowering himself from the hatch coaming, he found his second foothold. Now the smell was appalling, rising in waves around the descending policeman. Down and down, Halfhyde's lantern casting its flickering shadows ... it was like a descent into a tomb, and in all conscience it was not far from such, Todhunter thought. Never had he been in such a position, fearful every moment of falling to a nasty death to join the poor remains beneath. But at long, long last Halfhyde's lantern came to shoulder height and Todhunter's reaching foot touched bottom.

Trembling, Todhunter let go of the handhold above him and turned to face Halfhyde.

'A nasty place, I do declare,' he said in a shaking voice.

'Nastier than usual,' Halfhyde said. 'Look about you, Mr Todhunter.'

He lifted the lamp higher: the cable locker looked like a charnel house. Lumps of maggot-infested flesh were strewn about; broken, severed and naked limbs were to be seen. Wedged into the cable clench itself was what looked like a shattered head: hair, brain matter, dried blood, and no face left.

'As I said, Mr Todhunter. No identification possible.'

'No papers, Captain Halfhyde?'

'I can't say yet. As you see, however, there is clothing.'

92

'Yes, indeed.' Todhunter looked at tattered material, tweedy stuff he believed. There might be some identification. Todhunter swallowed: it would, of course, be his job to sift through everything in a search for clues.

Halfhyde said, 'You'll want everything left here, I take it. Evidence could be destroyed if I brought hands down to remove the pieces to the deck.'

'Yes. Yes, indeed, Captain Halfhyde.'

iii

Victoria was on the master's deck. As Halfhyde came up the ladder she held her nose tightly. Halfhyde glowered at her. He said, 'An unnecessary gesture—'

'It's bloody not, mate! It's not meant to be disrespectful of the dead, either.'

'You've heard, have you?'

She said promptly, 'Galley rumours. True, is it?'

'Yes.'

'What are you going to do about it?'

He shrugged. 'Wait for Todhunter's report. He's down there now.'

'Poor little sod,' she said sympathetically. 'Sooner him than me! After that, what?'

'I can't say yet. There's one thing sure, though: whatever Todhunter has to say about it, the remains go overboard as soon as he's finished!'

'A proper sea burial?'

'Sea committal,' he corrected. 'What else? It was once a human body.' He paused, looking around the decks: neither Wainscott nor Mayhew had turned up while the cable locker was being investigated. 'Have you seen Wainscott, Victoria?'

'He came up while you were busy. Said he'd leave you to it till you'd finished. Said he'd keep that Mayhew away too.'

Halfhyde nodded. Mayhew would have been the last straw. He said, 'He'll want a word, but he'll have to wait a little longer, while I have a wash down on deck.' Halfhyde called for Barsett; a wash-deck hose was to be rigged in the after well-deck. He went down the ladder and strode aft, then stripped off his clothing and threw it down to lie in a heap on the deck. One of the hands, sent for by Barsett, came along with a canvas hose which was connected to the sea-water pump. Halfhyde stood naked as the hose washed him down, washed away all traces of the stench from the cable locker. Victoria watched from above: Halfhyde's body was a good one, with lean limbs and torso burned a dark brown where they had met many a sun over the years at sea. No fat anywhere: accustomed as she was to his nakedness she was able to feel a reaction in her own body as she watched. When the hose was turned off Halfhyde came back and climbed the ladder.

Fresh clothing had been laid ready in his cabin. He sent Barsett down with a message to Commander Wainscott; and while he was dressing the naval officer arrived. Halfhyde made his apologies for not having been available sooner.

'A necessary ablution, Commander!'

'No doubt,' Wainscott said drily. 'Nasty business, Halfhyde. Have you any ideas?'

Halfhyde pulled a shirt over his head and spoke from within the clean linen. 'Not many as yet. Only that the body must have been put down into the cable locker in Liverpool, since we have no men missing to account for a corpse!'

'Or Funchal?'

'Funchal?' Halfhyde gave a hard laugh. 'I doubt it! Why bring a body aboard, even if it were possible, which—'

'At that stage, it might not have been a body.'

'True, but a clumsy way to commit a murder, I fancy!'

'But Liverpool ...' Wainscott spread his hands. 'When your watchman was being looked for—was there no inspection of the cable locker in Liverpool?'

'There was not,' Halfhyde said shortly. 'Perhaps there should have been.'

'Undoubtedly there should have been, as now we know.'

'The responsibility is mine alone,' Halfhyde

95

said.

Wainscott demurred. 'The police—'

'I am the Master of the *Taronga Park*. I should have seen to it that the cable locker was opened up.'

There was a silence as Halfhyde finished dressing. When dressed he called for his steward, who had been hovering in the pantry next to the cabin. 'Whisky, Barsett. Two glasses, if it's not too early for you, Commander?'

Wainscott said, 'In the circumstances, no.'

The whisky came. Halfhyde took his with a minimum of water. He relished the drink, the first pull at the glass cleansing away the taste of death that was still in his mouth. Wainscott held his glass up to the light coming through the port. It struck gold from the liquor. The naval officer had a quizzical look as he stared into it. He said, 'This will have to be reported, Halfhyde. To the Admiralty, I think, in the first instance. Then the Liverpool police.'

'It depends on Todhunter's report.'

Wainscott pursed his lips. 'There may be trouble with Mayhew. He'll want a degree of secrecy, which is why I suggested the Admiralty first. Mayhew's bound to see a connection with the Amazon.'

Halfhyde shrugged. 'We have nothing to go on unless we can obtain an identification. In any case, no report can be made until we reach the land and a wireless station, and that may not be before we make contact with our consul at Santarem.'

Wainscott nodded and took another mouthful of whisky. They sat in silence for a while, each thinking his own thoughts, Halfhyde cursing himself for not having had the cable locker investigated whilst in Liverpool. It had quite simply never occurred to him, nor apparently had it occurred to the Liverpool police—nor, at that stage, to Commander Wainscott either. It was easy to be wise after the event; but Halfhyde recognized his own culpability and would not step aside from it.

They had finished their whisky when there was a sound from the deck outside and a moment later a tap at the cabin doorpost. The curtain was pushed aside and Detective Inspector Todhunter entered. There was a strong smell; and Todhunter himself was swaying and looking very ill. He steadied himself against the doorpost.

'Well, Mr Todhunter. I think you're much in need of a stimulant,' Halfhyde said.

'Thank you, sir, I will not partake—'

'Nonsense! You've well deserved a moment's forgetfulness of your principles, man!'

Todhunter raised a shaking hand and brushed sweat from his forehead. 'No more than a cup of tea—'

Halfhyde called again for Barsett. Todhunter

removed his bowler hat and came right into the cabin. He was extremely agitated. He said, 'My hat, sir. It ... fell into—questionable matter.'

'Throw it outside at once, then,' Halfhyde snapped.

'Yes, perhaps I'd better,' Todhunter said. He went out to the deck and deposited the hat safely against the bulkhead of the cabin, wedging it behind an iron pipe. It was going to need disinfecting, which would not do the material any good. He went back in and accepted the tea brought by Barsett.

Halfhyde said, 'Now your report, if you please, Mr Todhunter.'

'Yes, sir.' Todhunter brought out his handkerchief and carefully wiped his lips. 'I carried out a very minute examination, gentlemen, of the—the remains and the clothing. Had I had the advantage, which I had not, needless to say—'

'Yes, yes!'

'—of a forensic expert or a medical gentleman,' Todhunter went on doggedly, 'it might have been possible to render a fuller report. But I had just to do my best in the circumstances, as my Chief Super would have expected—'

'And your conclusions, Mr Todhunter?'

'Murder had been committed, sir. Of that there was no doubt whatsoever. This I was able to deduce from the hypothesis that no person would have been able to open up the hatch into the cable locker, enter, and then shut the hatch again from the inside. Not, that is, without connivance. I refer, as you will have judged, gentlemen, to the fact that suicide can be ruled out.'

'For God's sake, Mr Todhunter!'

The detective inspector looked pained. 'It's my job, sir, to consider *all* possibilities. Each has to be gone into and then ruled out if the facts fail to fit. As in this case they do. Murder, then, by person or persons unknown.' There was a curious earnestness about the detective inspector, a simple honesty of purpose, a strong aura of sheer conscientiousness that kept Halfhyde silent. 'Now we come to the question of identity. The question, gentlemen, of who the victim was. In that regard I had more luck. If you can call it luck, that is. Oh, lumme, gentlemen, there's going to be a very great deal of trouble coming up and that's a fact!' Once again Todhunter wiped at his face, which had the aspect of melting butter.

'Let us have it,' Halfhyde said impatiently.

'Very well, sir. The clothing was badly shredded. There was some paper but that also was shredded and unreadable. Mostly, that is, I did, however, come upon a name, what appeared to be a surname, on a piece of paper somewhat damaged by seawater from the cable. I have this paper with me.' Todhunter reached into a pocket of the blue serge suit and brought out something which he handed to Wainscott. He looked expectantly at the naval officer. 'Peixoto, as you will see, sir. I suggest that Peixoto may be a Brazilian name.'

'A Brazilian, in Liverpool?' Wainscott raised his eyebrows.

Halfhyde said, 'Not particularly unusual.'

'Perhaps not. Certainly the nationality fits. I don't like this, Todhunter. Have you any theories?'

'Well, sir, I do believe the body was in fact Brazilian. Or at any rate South American or such—the pigmentation of the skin so far as I could make it out. Of course, that could be due to the deterioration. The putrefaction.'

'Indeed it could,' Halfhyde said drily.

'But the hair. That was undoubtedly dark. Black, indeed.' Todhunter coughed. 'The head and other parts—my investigation was thorough. And that, gentlemen, brings me to another aspect, one that I must admit greatly surprises me though as a detective inspector of the Yard I am not easily surprised. You yourselves, gentlemen, would be astonished at the great variety of experiences with which I have been confronted—'

'Quite so, Mr Todhunter.'

'I would hazard a guess—'

'The facts, if you please, Mr Todhunter. The air is thick. It is time you went beneath the

100

seawater pump.'

Todhunter flushed. 'Very well, sir. Beg pardon.' He took a deep breath before proceeding. 'The body, gentlemen, and never mind the clothing, which was male, no stays, no whalebone—was *not* that of a man. It was that of a woman.'

Halfhyde and Wainscott stared. Halfhyde said, 'A woman dressed as a man ... are you certain, Mr Todhunter? And if you are, may I ask how? The body was virtually in fragments, was it not?'

'Yes, indeed so, Captain Halfhyde, sir, it was. Oh, I had my work cut out I must confess! But I referred to the fact that I was very thorough.' Todhunter paused. 'There were indications, you see—'

'Breasts?'

'Not *intact* as such, sir, no.' Todhunter's voice became a little prim. 'I formed the impression that the lady had been flat-chested. Without going into great detail, sir, I had perhaps better correct my earlier statement—'

'Which one?'

'The one in which I referred to indications. I should have said that at first there was a *lack* of indications. If you get my meaning, gentlemen. Then I did discover something positive.' Todhunter brought out his handkerchief and to cover his embarrassment blew his nose with a sound like a trumpet. 'A female ... er. To my

101

mind, gentlemen, the fact of the female sex being involved complicates matters enormously. I think we should all approach Mr Mayhew for his advice.'

Wainscott asked, 'Why Mr Mayhew?'

'Well, sir, because there was a matter that was told to me in confidence by my Chief Super before I was despatched from the Yard to join this ship. A matter to which the Foreign Office was party. I shall now be obliged to come out into the open, as it might be said. But I prefer Mr Mayhew to be present. I have my career to consider, gentlemen. I trust you will understand.'

CHAPTER SEVEN

'No cock?' Victoria asked some while later.

'Apparently not.'

'It's a small enough thing—I mean, small enough to get bloody missed after a body's been shredded up, isn't it? Could have got crushed, I reckon, couldn't it?'

'Yes, I dare say—'

'I don't reckon it's conclusive, not by a long bloody chalk, mate!' The girl gave a shrill laugh. 'That Todhunter!'

Halfhyde said patiently, 'He's not basing his whole theory on what was missing, Victoria. He found something else which constituted more positive proof.'

'Mean he found a—'

'Yes,' Halfhyde said. 'Or I believe that was what he was getting at. Todhunter at times is full of circumlocutions.'

'Would he recognize one?' Victoria asked.

Halfhyde said gravely, 'In the line of duty, yes. It's not the first body he's seen, you know. I think we can assume he's got it right.'

Victoria nodded. 'Maybe. Could only be one or the other, right? He's got a fifty per cent chance, I'll say that.' She looked at Halfhyde narrowly. 'You were a long while with that ponce, weren't you?'

'Which ponce?'

'Mayhew.'

'I wouldn't let him hear you call him that, Victoria.'

'Why not? I don't give a fish's tit what that bloke thinks of me. Know something, do you?' She sniffed. 'He can't bloody wait to get a hand up. Stands out a bloody mile every time he looks at me with his bloody squint. Only hope is, being boss-eyed he might bloody miss the target . . .'

ii

Earlier, Mayhew's squint had criss-crossed the cabin as he spoke to Halfhyde and Wainscott about Todhunter's hitherto confidential knowledge. Put briefly, it appeared that the Foreign Office had received information, and Mayhew refused resolutely to indicate the source, that the Germans had been employing a woman to discover the British Government's intentions in South America. That alone, Mayhew said, was proof that the Germans had what he called a guilty conscience.

'And knowledge that they've been rumbled,' Wainscott said.

'Not necessarily, Commander. They may just be probing.'

'It's a pity the Admiralty was never informed. Why tell Scotland Yard and not us?'

Mayhew shrugged. 'The Admiralty, Commander ... estimable people, of course, but largely, in the senior ranks, men of the sea. Simple sailormen, not accustomed to the intrigues and diplomatic manoeuvres that go hand-in-hand with what one might call counter-espionage—'

'On that I agree with you,' Wainscott said tartly. 'We're not accustomed to lies and deceit, most certainly, except perhaps for the civil side. Why could not the First Lord have been taken into your confidence?'

Mayhew shrugged. 'It's not up to me to answer that, Commander, and I shall not do so. I prefer not to be pressed further on matters of state security. To get back to the point at issue, I find myself in full agreement with Todhunter that matters have taken a more serious turn. With the discovery of the woman's body, don't you know.'

'Is it your woman?' Halfhyde asked directly.

Mayhew squinted towards Halfhyde, taking in Todhunter at the same time. 'She should not be referred to as "my woman", Halfhyde. But to answer the purport of your question: yes, I think it likely enough. Anything else would be a coincidence too large to be acceptable. What we have to determine, of course, is what she was doing aboard and how she got into the, er, whatever you call it in the bows of the ship. Also why she was murdered. And I think I have the answers to all three of these questions.'

Mayhew proceeded to expound. The woman had gone aboard to snoop while the *Taronga Park* was without a crew. Somehow she had evaded the watchman, who, if the boarding had taken place at night particularly, could have been skulking, taking a nap under cover from Liverpool's interminable rain. What had she expected to find? Well, anything and everything was grist to the mill of a foreign spy, a dago in the pay of the German Emperor. She had had the ill luck to fall in with the other marauder, later the body in the chart room, and had been murdered by him. This unknown man, who could, in retrospect, have been a simple robber seeking pickings aboard a deserted ship, had opened up the cable locker and dumped the body in.

'It sounds too simple,' Halfhyde said.

'Large matters are often simple. You would agree, Todhunter?'

'Oh yes, indeed I would, sir. Very, very often! Why, I remember when I was once investigating a crime, a crime involving the murder of a prostitute in Hyde Park—'

'And in any case such conclusions as we may come to between us can be no more than guesswork. Do you agree with *that*, Mr Todhunter?'

Todhunter gave a sage nod. 'Why yes, sir, I do. I am forced to. There is no evidence to go upon, none at all.'

'Mr Mayhew?'

Mayhew blew out his cheeks and shook his head slowly from side to side as though wondering how much more of his private knowledge should now be revealed. After a longish pause he said, 'Yes, I agree. However, the name Peixoto introduces what may prove to be another factor. We in the Foreign Office were never given any name in connection with the woman said to be acting as a spy. But Peixoto, now—not a common name in Brazil—'

'It could be a false identity, sir,' Todhunter broke in.

'Yes. And are we *certain* that the name you found is in fact the name or pseudonym of the woman in the cable locker? I think the answer is

106

no, Todhunter. There is nothing positive to link that scrap of paper with the woman's identity. It could be part of a letter, could it not, with a reference in it to a third party?'

'Well, that's true, sir,' Todhunter admitted, looking somewhat abashed.

'We must avoid jumping to conclusions, then. All we are certain of is that the body was that of a woman—we have your word for that, Todhunter. Her name may or may not be Peixoto. However, if it is, it may be of some significance. I say—and I stress—*may be*. There could be a coincidence.' Mayhew paused. 'Peixoto. There was a Marshal Floriana Peixoto who was acting president of Brazil from 1891 to 1894. Not so long ago, you'll agree. He was known to be on friendly terms with the German Emperor and to have much encouraged trade between his country and Germany—this may be of no present relevance, perhaps, but I find it interesting. The more so since I myself know of the name Peixoto in another connection: Marshal Peixoto's niece.'

'Yes?' Wainscott asked.

'She is—or should we say was?—said to be a woman of beauty. Seductive, I understand.'

'The seductive spy?' Commander Wainscott's tone verged on the derisive: he had been annoyed by Mayhew's slighting reference to seafarers. 'Do such, in fact, exist—and if they do, would they be employed in the form of pilferers and—'

'I have not suggested for one moment that the woman of whom I speak is either a spy or is the woman from the cable locker, Commander. I merely state such facts as I know about a woman named Peixoto. Maria Peixoto. Strictly between the four of us, Maria Peixoto—the knowledge reached Whitehall by a clandestine route—has for some time been the mistress of our consul in Santarem.'

Mayhew had dropped a bombshell and knew it. His eyes held a crafty look of triumph, of the man who has taken the attention of the court. He would say no more on the point, preferring, he said, not to speculate, for speculation until more was known could lead to false conclusions. He would agree only that if the dead woman was in fact Maria Peixoto then it was possible that the British consul in Santarem might have to be considered not wholly trustworthy in the current situation.

The discussion continued along other lines, of ways and means to proceed once the *Taronga Park* had entered the waters of the Amazon. When it became evident that little progress was being made, Halfhyde got to his feet and said the sun was high, and there was to be no more delay in disposing of the contents of the cable locker.

Bosun Taggart detailed three hands and went down with them into the cable locker. Halfhyde had asked Todhunter formally whether or not he had finished with the remnants of flesh and clothing: Todhunter had. There was nothing he could do and he had taken copious notes.

'My Chief Super—he's very strict on notes. Very strict.'

It took the fo'c'sle hands little more than half an hour to scrape up the remains and put them in a canvas bag and then clean up the cable locker with salt water. When they emerged they went to the side and were sick. Halfhyde sent Barsett for'ard with whisky and at the same time passed the order to the First Mate to heave in on the windlass and bring the anchor once again to the cathead. Before the ship got under way again he made for his cabin and brought a Bible from his safe. Then, with Wainscott, Mayhew and Todhunter, he went to the fore well-deck where a seaman was standing by the canvas bag. At a word from Halfhyde the man lifted the bag to the bulwarks. Halfhyde read a shortened form of the committal service and without further ceremony the bag was dropped over the side to take the water with a splash. Halfhyde, his hands clasped behind his back, walked aft past the cargo hatch and climbed to the bridge. A few minutes later Briggs reported the anchor aweigh.

'Thank you, Mr Briggs. Mr Harrison, the engine to slow ahead.'

'Slow ahead, sir.' The Second Mate pulled over the handle of the telegraph and water began to boil up beneath the counter. The *Taronga Park* moved ahead; as the anchor broke surface and was heaved in for catting, Halfhyde increased speed to full and the thump-thump of the engines reverberated again throughout the ship and the thick black smoke swirled down over the bridge before the wind, which now had a shade more weight in it.

As the day wore on that wind increased still more: the sky dulled with heavy cloud and the sea's surface grew ruffled until it was covered with breaking waves and, as night came down, spindrift was blown from aft to fling over the engineers' accommodation and bring wet to the after well-deck and the canvas-covered hatch. Mr Mayhew, coming for'ard to the saloon for his dinner, was taken by a heavy shower of spray and with an oath retreated back to the shelter of the alleyway. Mr Todhunter, as the ship's motion increased with some violence, sought his panacea in his cabin and shook out two tablets from the bottle; these, for him, would be that night's dinner. He was still distressed about his bowler hat, from which the odour had not all been washed away and which resembled a drowned cat, the nap in a most terrible state.

With his ship in the capable hands of Briggs, Halfhyde was in his usual place in the saloon, with Wainscott on his left and Chief Engineer Bannion at the other end of the table. Bannion was a morose man who normally carried a smell of whisky around with him, a little less at sea than in port; and he said little but ate steadily of whatever was set before him by the steward. Victoria Penn sat at Halfhyde's right hand, unusually silent: the day's events had been dampening to the spirit. Somewhat late, Mayhew turned up, a trifle wet despite the cloak he had gone back to fetch.

'Stormy, Captain Halfhyde.'

'Tending that way certainly.'

Mayhew sat down with a grunt. Seamen had little sensitivity and no sympathy: to Mayhew, the ship was already *in extremis*. 'Will it grow worse, do you think?'

'Yes,' Halfhyde said. 'The glass is dripping, and the wind's veering. If it veers right round, as I suspect it may, we shall find ourselves driving right into it. If it doesn't go so far, we shall take a nasty beam sea.'

'But we shall be safe?' Mayhew looked with distaste at what he had been told was sea pie, a nasty concoction of broken ship's biscuit and corned beef from a tin.

'Yes.'

Mayhew squinted at him from under his shaggy brows. He seemed confident, Mayhew

111

thought, not in the least anxious. Well, that was good, of course, but ships had been lost before now. Over confidence? Surely a shipmaster ought to be on the bridge and not calmly dining in the saloon? The sea was very rough now; Mayhew's mind roved over all the past sea disasters he could remember. There had been so many. Lloyd's of London—they were always ringing the Lutine bell to announce bad news for the brokers carrying bottom insurance, vast sums of money lost—and lives! There was a bottle of whisky on the saloon table, in a coaster that had already slid with the roll of the ship to the fiddley that ran like a bulwark around the table's edge to prevent things falling off. Mayhew reached for the bottle. Halfhyde watched sardonically, but said nothing as the diplomat poured himself a strong glass, taking little water for it. Sometimes whisky was a help to seasickness, sometimes it was not. It depended on the person, the stomach and the food taken. Mayhew's first drink was purely precautionary; the second was taken because he liked it. The glow was good. Halfhyde, his own meal finished, excused himself and left the saloon, followed by Commander Wainscott and a little later by Bannion. Mayhew took a third whisky and smiled across the table at Victoria.

'Better take it easy, mate,' the girl said.

'Mate? I don't—'

'Term of endearment,' Victoria said.

'Sometimes.'

'Yes, I see.' Mayhew gave a cough. 'Would you care to join me, Miss Penn?'

'Join you, eh? In what?'

'A drink.'

She shook her head. 'No, thanks. I don't drink whisky. Gin, yes. Ever heard of Vicker's gin?'

'Er . . . no, I—'

'Australian. Puts hairs on your chest.' She giggled.

'Really.' Mayhew gave a cough and stroked his chin thoughtfully. She was a vulgar young woman, of course, but could what she had said represent some sort of advance? It was possible; in an English young lady it could be construed no other way, but Australians were different, they were all rather common and all rather forthright too. Mayhew poured another whisky. The girl was certainly in no hurry to leave the table and Todhunter, charged with his particular duty, was not present to do it. It would be foolish, of course, to give way too far to opportune proximity, but he was not, after all, contemplating actual rape even though desire was strong. He had always understood that funny things were forgotten as soon as land hove in sight and women returned to normal. And there were always strings he could pull against anyone inclined to talk. There was, of course, Halfhyde, of whom the girl was

obviously fond—indeed, whose mistress she
was. But a woman of easy virtue, brazen, a
hussy . . . faint heart, Mayhew reflected, never
won fair lady. And Halfhyde was a mere sailor.
The touch of the Foreign Office might not come
amiss. Mayhew coughed again.

'It's the sea air,' Victoria said.

'What is?'

'That cough.' She knew perfectly well what
was in the diplomat's mind and she was far
from worried as his gaze crossed over her
breast. 'That why you're getting yourself
pissed, is it, mate?'

'Really, I—'

'Sorry for me language,' she said pertly. 'It's
because I'm a bloody Aussie, that's all.'

'Yes, quite.'

'Speak me mind.'

Mayhew edged closer and slid a hand along
the table until it rested next to Victoria's arm.
She looked down at it; it was soft and white,
unlike Halfhyde's hard bone and weathered
skin. It gave her an attack of the creeps. There
was now what appeared to be a leer in
Mayhew's eyes: they were glassy and his hand
had dropped beneath the table. A moment later
she felt it on her thigh. Her reaction was
instant: her thigh came up hard and smashed
the hand against the underside of the table.
Mayhew gave a cry of pain and surprise.

'Watch it, mate,' Victoria said. She laughed.

'But it wouldn't have been any bloody good anyhow. Soft half inch in the middle if you ask me. Ever heard of whisky prick?'

iv

By midnight there was a full gale blowing and, as Halfhyde had predicted, the wind had veered to the south-east. The *Taronga Park* was taking a heavy sea on her port quarter; the motion was a nasty twisting one as the ship pitched and rolled at the same time. It made Mr Todhunter, miserable in his tiny cabin, think of corkscrews. Dr Datchet was failing him and he was producing green bile each time he rose from his bunk to approach his wash-basin. Thumps and bangs and crashes came from all around, above and below, reminding him of the frailty of even large ships in stormy weather. If this went on they must founder. Lost at sea with all hands, what a fate! Not that he would mind at this moment—death would come as a friend. In an attempt to keep his mind busy so that his stomach would not obtrude, Mr Todhunter did his best to reflect upon his duty and his current mission to uphold the British law in heathen parts. But all that this produced was the cable locker and its contents, and the smell, and he became much worse. His stomach was raw; he was bringing up his very bowels. The ship rose and then fell back with a swoop, Mr Todhunter's stomach remaining for a moment suspended above him from the deckhead, until it dropped like lightning and sped past his ears, again and again, like a game of ping-pong with his stomach the ball.

He began to pray aloud. God had once calmed the raging of the Sea of Galilee. He could do the same for the wretched North Atlantic. Every now and again, each time the stern rose high to the pounding waves and the surge beneath the hull, there was an appalling shudder and vibration and a terrible sound of machinery in torment, and God could do something about that at the same time.

From the engine-room Mr Bannion, by-passing God, called the bridge via the voice-pipe. Halfhyde answered: he was keeping the bridge while the weather lasted. 'Bridge, Captain speaking.'

'Chief here. Screw's racing.'

'I realize that, Chief. Any damage?'

'Not yet, no. But if it goes on the vibration could start some plates.'

Alternately ear and mouth to the voice-pipe, Halfhyde fought against the shriek of the wind and the thunder of the seas dropping aboard along the port side. He shouted into the pipe that if Bannion thought it necessary he would alter to the south-east and put the ship's head into wind and sea, which would hold her steadier. Bannion's voice came back: the ship was no longer young. Some easement would be an advantage.

Halfhyde called to the Second Mate. 'Bring her round, Mr Harrison—round to port, and steer south-east.'

'Aye, aye, sir.'

The order went to the helmsman. Slowly the *Taronga Park* came round to her new course, the wind and sea coming onto the port bow for a while as she swung, sending her stem over in a heavy lurch. Spray shot high and was blown back over the bridge, drenchingly. In the dim light from the binnacle Halfhyde's oilskins shone eerily. Round she came until her head was pointing into the wind and sea. Solid water came over the fo'c'sle-head to drop down onto the windlass and the cover of the fore hatch, ton upon ton of flinging water, but now she rode easier, held to the wind, with a steadier motion, and the screw was less frequently lifted from the water to spin wildly in the empty air. Face to the wind, Halfhyde stared out ahead. The alteration of course was going to mean time lost; how much depended on how long the gale lasted. Soon after the ship had steadied, Commander Wainscott, alerted as any seaman by the change in the motion, came to the bridge.

'You've altered, Halfhyde.'

'As you can see.'

'Let's hope it doesn't last. The Admiralty won't want delay.'

'Or the Foreign Office?'

Halfhyde saw the naval officer's teeth flash white in a grin. 'The Foreign Office has currently lost interest, I fear! Mayhew's as drunk as a fiddler's bitch. His cabin door had come open as I passed on my way up here.'

Halfhyde said, 'He started at dinner.'

'I know. And he has a supply in his cabin, I fancy.'

'He's in his bunk?'

'No. Splayed out in a chair, staring into space both ways at once. I wouldn't have thought it was like him.' Wainscott paused. 'I wonder what's done it?'

Halfhyde grinned. 'I think his pride's been hurt.' He didn't embellish; Victoria's report had been graphic but was not to be repeated. For his part Wainscott was still curious and seemed about to press when Halfhyde's attention was caught by something out-of-place below in the fore well-deck: a corner of the canvas cover had come adrift and was flapping about in the tearing wind. More of the cover was coming away; if it went, the planks could be started and the hold would fill with water. Halfhyde acted instantly.

'Mr Harrison, get below and rouse out the bosun and all hands to secure the fore hatch. I'll take the ship myself.'

He stepped to the binnacle while Harrison went down the ladder fast, sliding his hands down the rail, and fought his way through wind and water for the door into the fo'c'sle accommodation. Halfhyde heard his shout from inside the alleyway, and within the next half minute the hands were turning out, pulling on oilskins and sou'westers as they emerged into the open, into the gale's fury and the dim glow from the steaming lights. Halfhyde heard the bosun urging them to make haste, and then saw the tarpaulin lift with a tearing sound and whip clear away into the night. A moment later a huge sea came over the fo'c'sle to smash down into the well-deck and send the men flying along the deck to fetch up against the bulwarks. Solid water rushed aft, the air was filled with spray. As Taggart scrambled to his feet Halfhyde heard his shout.

'Watch that plank, there! Where's the bleeding chippy?'

Halfhyde saw the carpenter jump up onto the hatch, and saw a plank lift and come free, its end rising to the rush and tumble of another heavy sea. It flew away into the night and there was a shout of pain from for'ard. By this time the First Mate had come to the bridge; he saw the situation and without waiting for orders slid down the ladder to take charge at the fore hatch. As the wind and sea got a grip beneath the planks more were coming free: the hold would be shipping a lot of water, far too much for the pumps to be of any use until the weather

119

moderated. The risk was great: Halfhyde balanced it against the risk, a lesser one as he saw it, of being pooped if he turned the ship again so that her stern was presented to the wind and sea.

Using a megaphone he called down to the well-deck.

'Mr Briggs!'

'Aye, sir?'

'I'm altering to starboard. We'll run before the wind.'

'Aye, aye, sir. I'm getting more canvas brought up, sir, but it'll not keep all the water out.'

'Just do your best, Mr Briggs.'

Halfhyde went back to the binnacle and passed the helm order. Slowly the *Taronga Park* came round to starboard, bringing the wind once again abeam to send her hard over, lurching horribly as she fell into the trough of the waves—the moment of greatest danger in which she might broach-to, unable to make headway to port or starboard to climb the crests, and lie helpless beneath the batter of the beam seas. Halfhyde stood like a statue at the bridge rail, the heavy spray flying past his tall figure as he watched and waited, and joined the bunk-bound detective inspector in a prayer for his ship's safety.

She came round, protestingly and with a devilish din from below as more gear shifted to

120

the appalling roll. Halfhyde let out a sigh of relief as at last she steadied with the wind and sea dead astern. He used the voice-pipe to the engine-room.

'All speed you can muster, if you please, Mr Bannion.'

There was a grunt from the voice-pipe: Bannion liked to tend his engine. But he would know the urgency: it was vital that the ship be kept ahead of the following sea, or the after hatch could go the same way as the fore hatch. Halfhyde looked along the decks. Conditions had eased considerably for'ard and the Second Mate with the bosun were supervising the rigging of a new tarpaulin over the hatch. Other hands under Briggs were making their way aft with difficulty to rig an extra tarpaulin as a precaution over the after hatch. Then just a moment later the sea manifested more of its power to destroy: there was a sudden cry from aft and as Halfhyde swung round he caught a brief glimpse of a figure flying through the air, taken as it seemed by a sudden whipping of the new tarpaulin that had thrown him clear over the bulwarks.

Briggs' shout cut along the gale: 'Man overboard port!'

Halfhyde felt the clench of his fists, the bite of nails into palms. No crew could get a boat away in such weather, to order it would be an act of murder. To stop engines with such a following sea was to invite worse danger for ship and crew. Halfhyde was aware of Wainscott at his side. He said, 'There's nothing I can do, Commander.'

'I know. Don't blame yourself. I understand. We're both seamen, Halfhyde.'

v

Briggs had done what he could: a grass line had been cast and trailed astern but was useless. No hand came up to grasp it, nothing was seen again. The *Taronga Park* moved on, the work proceeded on the fore hatch. As soon as the new tarpaulin had been rigged and double-banked the pumps were started. Thanks to quick action there was not a lot of water in the hold; by the time a watery dawn came up the pumps had done their job, and the ship was riding easier in the remnant of a gale that had largely blown itself out during the rest of the night. The man who had gone was one of the naval party who had come to the assistance of the ship's crew. The gunner's mate had come to the bridge to report, his face sombre.

'I'm very sorry,' Halfhyde said. 'The poor fellow had no particular duty to my ship. I thank you all for your assistance.' That was all; there was no more he could say. All seamen were aware of the risks from the moment they joined the Queen's service or the merchantmen. But later that day, as the sun came up in a clearing sky and the *Taronga Park* resumed her course for the Amazon River, Halfhyde noted a changed feeling in the air. There had been a body in the cable locker, following two murders on board in Liverpool—and now a man lost to the power and fury of the sea. The *Taronga Park* was in danger of becoming a voodoo ship, a ship of ill fortune, bound away upon a doomed mission. Seamen were always superstitious, especially about deaths aboard. It had seemed to affect even Victoria. When Halfhyde went below at last, she was pensive and moody.

'It's bloody bad, mate.'

He had a flash of anger. 'Are you blaming me?'

'Course not. Except for agreeing to the bloody charter in the first place.' She shivered. 'But I don't like it and that's dinkum.'

CHAPTER EIGHT

There was already the feeling of the shore ahead by the time the masthead lookout reported their first landfall. Halfhyde acknowledged the man's shout and lifted his telescope. Slowly, as the *Taronga Park* moved on to bring the landfall within range from the bridge, he made out the approaches to the river. He handed the

123

telescope to the First Mate.

'Now, Mr Briggs, let us have evidence of your local knowledge. Can you identify anything ahead there?'

Briggs took a long look through the telescope. 'A good landfall, sir. Cape Maguarhino dead ahead.'

'And distant about twelve miles?'

'Aye, sir, about that.'

Halfhyde took back the telescope and snapped it shut. 'We shall alter to starboard as we approach, Mr Briggs, and enter by the Canal Perigoso. You shall take the ship.'

Briggs was pleased. 'Why, thank you, sir—'

'You have the local knowledge which I have not. I shall remain on the bridge. You shall act as pilot.' Halfhyde had decided some while ago that he would not entrust his ship to the local pilotage. If a pilot offered his services he would be embarked and his advice listened to; but on no account would he be allowed the actual handling of the *Taronga Park*, which would be a bigger ship than was normal for the river. As they moved towards the shoreline and the great wide mouth of the Amazon, and picked up the unmistakable smell of the land wafting out along an off-shore breeze, Halfhyde's mind went back over the last days of the outward voyage.

The crew had been in a surly mood; Petty Officer Parker had carried out his daily drills

124

with more than his usual bark and bite, and had been seen to cast an eye several times towards Victoria when she had been on deck. Victoria had reported the man's earlier advances but had been more amused than anything else: she could, she said, cope with that sort of thing. Mayhew had been largely silent, avoiding both Halfhyde and Victoria whenever possible, and meals in the saloon had been an obvious trial to him. He had tended to spend his time, when not alone, with Todhunter. A strange mixture, Halfhyde thought, a policeman and an official of the Foreign Office. Todhunter was perhaps flattered at friendliness from so august a source. Mayhew, without being too precise, had tended to give the impression that he was of high rank; Wainscott, also without being too precise, had hinted that Mayhew was not so high-ranking as he inferred, although to Wainscott the involved heirarchy of the Foreign Office was something of a closed book.

'As I've said before, Halfhyde, we're both plain men, both seamen.'

'Yes. But soon, I gather, to operate on land. Damn it, I've still no idea what we're supposed to do about the Germans!'

'It will become clearer after arrival, Halfhyde.' That was all Wainscott would say; indeed, he seemed on the whole disinclined to discuss the future and Halfhyde was left wondering if in fact he knew anything beyond the orders, such as they were, contained in the sealed envelopes. Now arrival was imminent, and Halfhyde's orders after entry were for the small port of Gurupá and the discharge of his cargo. From the Canal Perigoso to Gurupá was a distance of some hundred and fifty miles of tricky pilotage between the many islands, large and small, that dotted the channel.

ii

Victoria spent a good deal of the passage on the bridge with Halfhyde and the First Mate, fanning herself with a large straw bonnet.

'It's bloody stifling,' she said.

Halfhyde nodded: the air was close and foetid, strange smells arising from muddy waters as they threaded their way past thickly growing forests on either hand. It was an eerie progress, the more so the farther inland they penetrated from the open sea beyond the Canal Perigoso. Halfhyde had kept his engine dead slow once they had moved out of the comparatively wide waters inside the mouth itself: the channel narrowed very considerably after passing to the north of Afua and much care was necessary; but Briggs was cool and was proving his worth. As for Victoria, she was all eyes.

'Look, mate! What's that, eh?'

She pointed down the side. Something was floating past, head down in the water, a hump

126

of naked flesh. It was, Halfhyde said, a body.

'Thought so.' She gave a shiver. 'Reckon we've had enough bodies! Think he was murdered, do you?'

Halfhyde shrugged. 'Perhaps. Or carried away in a flood.'

'They used to find bodies in Sydney harbour—'

'I know. It's not unusual.'

'They were always murdered,' she said.

She didn't speak much after that. More things drifted past, dead animals, vegetation; and more smells came. With them during the next forenoon came Detective Inspector Todhunter, seeking information.

'Captain Halfhyde, sir. Would I be correct in thinking we are now not far off the port of Gurupá?'

'Quite correct, Mr Todhunter. I expect to make my arrival within two hours.'

'I see, sir.' Todhunter removed his bowler hat, now refurbished to his satisfaction by Barsett, and mopped at his forehead. 'I am ready, sir.'

Halfhyde raised an eyebrow. 'For what, Mr Todhunter?'

'Well, I—I'm not quite sure, sir, to be perfectly frank and honest. But I am ready to do my duty.'

'Good! You'll be informed the moment you're required, I assure you.'

'Thank you, sir.' The bowler hat was replaced. Todhunter looked hot and steamy in his blue serge suit. Even his moustache dripped sweat. It was on Halfhyde's lips to suggest that he shift into something more suitable to the Amazon, but he refrained: blue serge was probably the required rig at Scotland Yard, and everything about Todhunter said that where he himself was, so was Scotland Yard. 'In that case, sir, I shall go below, and keep out of the sun for so long as I can.'

'A good idea, Mr Todhunter.'

'My old mother, sir ... she once had too much of a touch of the sun. In Hyde Park it was. She came all over queer, sir, and lurched about, me not being with her at the time, and she was arrested. Of course, it came all right in the end, but—'

'You'll not want the same fate, Mr Todhunter, although the only person likely to arrest you here would be yourself. Follow your own suggestion, Mr Todhunter, and go below.'

Todhunter went down the ladder, leaving more space on the small bridge.

The *Taronga Park* moved on in a haze of almost overwhelming, enervating heat that left men drained and wearied before they had lifted a finger in the ship's working routine. Halfhyde, too hot even to pace the bridge, remained braced against the rail, watchful for the ship's safety as they came to shoaling water

128

with the Second Mate and a leadsman taking soundings ahead from the lifeboat that had been put in the water soon after passing Afua.

'Gurupá ahead, sir.'

Halfhyde nodded. 'Thank you, Mr Briggs.' He lifted his telescope. The port appeared only just worthy of the description: a wooden jetty, some low buildings in the rear, a rutted track leading from the jetty's end towards the west. Quizzing Briggs earlier, Halfhyde had established that although the chart showed there would be enough water to take the *Taronga Park* alongside, it would be more prudent to lie at anchor in the stream and discharge their cargo into boats from the shore. The jetty, Briggs had said, was a rickety affair and could be pulled over by any surge of the ship against her securing ropes. In such an event not only might the ship be in danger but her master would be presented with a bill for damaging the jetty.

As they came nearer there was a bustle around the buildings and a number of people were seen coming along the jetty.

'A reception committee, Mr Briggs?'

'Yes, sir—'

'A usual occurrence?'

'There's always an interest in an arrival at the river ports.'

Halfhyde nodded, then felt Commander Wainscott's hand on his shoulder. 'Your telescope, Halfhyde?' he asked.

Halfhyde handed it over. Wainscott studied the jetty and its occupants. Lowerng the telescope he said, 'I recognize one of them.'

'Who?'

'Millington.'

'Our consul at Santarem?' Halfhyde was surprised. 'Come for his cargo in person? I take it this was not expected?'

'By no means.' Wainscott sounded uneasy. 'We had better have Mayhew here, I fancy.' He grinned. 'The Foreign Office may have some views, and even if it hasn't it'll want to keep its fingers on the pulse of events!'

Mayhew was sent for; as it turned out he was on his way to the bridge already. He had, he said, a pair of binoculars and had seen the consul for himself. 'I have no idea why he's here, currently,' he said. 'I can suggest only that he may have orders. He is, after all, in touch with London by means of the ocean cable—'

'But not, as we know, from Santarem.'

'Not from Santarem. From Georgetown in British Guiana.'

'A long way, Mr Mayhew?'

Mayhew said irritably. 'There are messengers, Captain.' He added, 'Dedicated men, and highly trustworthy.'

130

Halfhyde shrugged; messengers would have to be very dedicated indeed to attempt the appalling cross-country journey of something like eight hundred miles, and the time taken would very largely negate the value of the cable in a period of emergency. To all intents and purposes Santarem was out of communication with London or anywhere else. While the diplomat went into a huddle with Commander Wainscott, Halfhyde passed the orders preparatory to anchoring off the port.

'Mr Briggs, I'll take the ship. Pass to the lifeboat, they're to come alongside to the davits for hoisting. Then stand by the anchor. I'll bring her up at three cables.'

'Aye, aye, sir.' Briggs went down the ladder and made his way to the fo'c'sle-head, calling for the bosun and the carpenter, the latter to take up his place at the windlass. Halfhyde, conning his ship to the anchorage, was fully engaged; Wainscott used the telescope again and studied the shore and the waiting people. Now, as the way came off the ship and the small disturbance of air made by her passage was lost, the heat lay like a blanket, pressing down and making even breathing difficult. Away to the south a line of heavy cloud lay, seemingly motionless in the total lack of wind.

A shout came from Halfhyde: 'Let go!'

From the fo'c'sle the First Mate, who had lifted an arm in readiness for the order, brought

131

it down sharply and at the windlass the carpenter took off the brake. With the anchor already freed of its slips and strops and hanging on the brake, the cable came up from the locker below in a cloud of red rust, the links banging and clattering in an appalling racket across the fo'c'sle until Briggs, watching the markings on the joining shackles as they flashed past to the hawse-pipe, signalled the carpenter to apply the brake. The sudden silence was as startling as the sudden noise had been to Mr Todhunter, watching from the after well-deck and wondering what exactly was coming up from the cable locker: the earlier search could possibly have missed a fragment or two, though he thought it unlikely. The First Mate's shout reached him from for'ard: 'Third shackle on deck, sir!'

The *Taronga Park* had arrived safely: well, that was something! A long voyage and at times an unpleasant one ... Todhunter wriggled uncomfortably, feeling sweat pour everywhere. What a terrible place. He had great sympathy for any white men who had to spend their working lives in such dreadful heat and humidity. He waited to do his duty when summoned and meanwhile listened to an exchange of shouts between Halfhyde and some person on the jetty. Halfhyde was indicating that he wished for boats to take off his cargo. Someone else was shouting back through a megaphone that he wished to come aboard. Soon after this Halfhyde called across the water that this person could come off in the first of the makeshift lighters, but the person protested that the Brazilian workers were lethargic and there might be a long wait. In the meantime there was urgency. Would Captain Halfhyde kindly send his own boat?

The lifeboat was called away again and lowered from the davits with the Second Mate in the sternsheets. Fifteen minutes later Todhunter watched a short, fat man wearing a white suit and a Panama hat embark, puffing and panting and very red in the face, from a Jacob's ladder cast over the port for'ard bulwarks.

iv

'Millington . . . British consul at Santarem. You are Captain Halfhyde?'

'I am, Mr Millington. Mr Mayhew, Commander Wainscott—'

'Ah yes, yes, we've met.' Millington, a pompous little man, looked temporarily disconcerted; and Halfhyde, remembering what Wainscott had said about him earlier, was able to guess why. 'You've arrived just about in time. That is, I hope you have. We must make all speed to Santarem—'

Halfhyde said, 'I have a cargo to discharge, Mr Millington.'

133

'Yes, yes, I'm aware of that. It must be carried on to Santarem. I did not wish to call this across the water, as I think you'll understand.' The consul stared up at Halfhyde. 'You'll also be aware that the consignee is myself. There will be no difficulty over changing your port of discharge. Now, Mr Mayhew, I think you'll agree that we should have a private discussion. You and I and Commander Wainscott.'

'Yes, indeed,' Mayhew said. 'I—'

'One moment.' Halfhyde's voice was crisp. 'As Master, there are things I must know—'

'You'll be told in due course.' Millington stared him up and down coolly, as though surveying a specimen in a glass case. 'All you're currently required to do is to take the ship up river to Santarem. *Immediately*. You understand? We cannot afford delay.'

Halfhyde's fists clenched and his mouth opened, then shut again. He must control his temper until he had Millington's measure at least. Mayhew, rubbing his hands together, urged the consul towards the ladder; going down behind them, Wainscott turned and gave Halfhyde an almost imperceptible wink. When the trio had passed out of earshot Victoria came across and took Halfhyde's hand.

'Don't give it a thought, mate. Little bugger! Any luck, a bloody crocodile'll get him one day.' She paused. 'Do we take it he's coming with us? To this bloody Santarem?'

'Unfortunately, yes. Unless he always uses the royal "we".'

'Come again?'

'Her Majesty Queen Victoria, Victoria. She is accustomed to refer to herself in the plural.'

'I always did reckon poms were loony.'

Halfhyde went to the fore rail of the bridge. 'Mr Briggs, see the lifeboat secured at the davits but to remain ready for lowering—davits swung out, if you please. Then stand by to weigh—and resecure the cargo hatches. We're moving up river immediately.' He went to the voice-pipe and warned the engine-room to stand by. Fifteen minutes later the *Taronga Park* moved out.

They had not long cleared the little port when Halfhyde noted a change in the temperature and felt a stirring of wind, little more so far than a welcome breeze. At the same time the distant line of cloud began to extend across the skyline and to reach out towards the river. Halfhyde knew the signs: there was going to be a deluge, but at least it was a shade cooler.

When a step came on the ladder and Wainscott appeared, the cloud had extended a good deal farther.

Wainscott sniffed the air. 'Oilskins again,' he said.

'Yes. What else is in the air, Commander?'

Wainscott frowned. 'I don't know.'

'But something is? Millington?'

'He's part of it, yes. Uncommunicative—and seems on edge. Unwelcoming. I don't think he expected such a positive response to that despatch of his.' Wainscott laughed. 'We may interfere, I suppose, with his happy routine, his drinking. He's been a little tin god in Santarem, I fancy, and we're the interlopers.'

'Has he further information about the Germans?'

'No. Not that he would say, that is. I got the impression he was playing it all down, in fact. It's possible the Admiralty has jumped the gun, I suppose.' Wainscott, however, didn't sound convinced of that.

'Or the Foreign Office has. Well—no doubt we shall see.' As Halfhyde spoke, the rain started. Just a few drops to begin with, heavy, falling in splodges on the bridge, and then, suddenly, a downpour so strong that as the raindrops hit the deck they bounced back up so that everyone in the open was soaked through in seconds, both from above and from below. They stood as if in a bath, and as the rain fell the temperature dropped farther. Halfhyde gave a shiver, but not from the sudden cooling. As a seaman he disliked being in narrow waters; the proximity of the jungle-covered shore was claustrophobic and threatening, and the unexpected arrival of the British consul was somehow adding to the tension. And a fraction before the heavens opened Halfhyde had glimpsed the movement in the trees along the river bank to starboard, the sudden and brief glitter of metal from a rifle.

CHAPTER NINE

The river journey to Santarem would take two days, perhaps a little more. Millington had been given accommodation aft, turning the second engineer out of his cabin to occupy the bunk of the third engineer when the latter was on watch below. The consul was appraising his quarters when the message reached him that a rifle had been seen.

He went for'ard grumpily and climbed the ladders to the bridge. 'What's all this?' he demanded.

'A rifle—'

'Yes, yes, so I'm told. Must be a mistake.'

'It was no mistake, I assure you.'

Millington was frigid. 'If I say it was a mistake, it was a mistake, Captain.'

'My dear sir, I saw—'

'There are no Germans within a hundred miles—two hundred miles—to my certain knowledge.'

'Possibly it was not a German, Mr Millington. No doubt Brazilians possess rifles.

There's probably no cause for alarm, but I thought you should be told.'

'H'm. Yes, if you really thought you saw a rifle, but we don't want any unnecessary alarms and excursions. You must remember the *Taronga Park* is a simple trading vessel, bound for Santarem to discharge cargo. The Germans must not get wind of anything deeper than that—there is no point in upsetting them, exacerbating anything. Among other things, the naval guard must on no account be seen whilst we are on passage. There is to be no question, for instance, of turning them out every time you think you see a rifle, Captain.'

Halfhyde restrained his rising temper. 'You appear much concerned for the Germans' feelings, Mr Millington.'

'I wish no bulls at gates, Captain. Diplomacy must be maintained, a balance struck between many national interests, not least the Brazilians. There are trading interests at stake, but I shall not go into that at this moment.'

Halfhyde shrugged. 'As you wish, of course.'

Millington turned away abruptly and made for the ladder. Halfhyde, on a sudden impulse, stopped his retreat by saying, 'Perhaps you know a body was found aboard my ship. Three bodies—two in Liverpool, one whilst at sea.'

'So I understand from Mr Mayhew.'

'It's possible the name of the body found at sea was Maria Peixoto.'

138

'Really.' Halfhyde had turned to observe the face: it was expressionless. 'That, too, I was told by Mayhew.'

'I was wondering if you—'

'It's no concern of mine, none at all.' Millington's voice was cold but under control. Halfhyde asked no further questions and Millington turned again and went down the ladder. Halfhyde stared after him, reflectively.

ii

'Whose side's he on, eh?' Victoria asked later.

'Ours, presumably.'

'Well,' she said flatly, 'from what you told me he doesn't bloody sound it, not to me.' She paused, frowning. 'Not but what I don't reckon you're *all* bloody twisters, mate! What's it to do with bloody Britain, what the Germans and Brazilians do among themselves, eh?'

'A question of patriotism,' Halfhyde said, sounding pompous even in his own ears.

'Even if we bloody interfere with other people?'

'Yes!'

'That's why I said you're all twisters!' She looked triumphant. 'I reckon this is an expedition to do the dirty without being bloody seen to do it, right? Only question is, how?'

Halfhyde didn't answer. He went back to the bridge, leaving Victoria alone in his cabin. The rain had stopped now but the atmosphere was heavy and damp, the decks gleaming wet. After a look at the chart Halfhyde told the First Mate he would take over; it was time for Briggs to get some sleep, and the ship had by now entered a fairly straightforward stretch of river. Standing braced against the fore rail, Halfhyde pondered. His was the responsibility for the ship; Wainscott, Mayhew and Millington would be responsible for the rest. And Todhunter? A misfit brought along as a kind of long stop? But Millington ... Halfhyde wondered about the total lack of reaction when he had mentioned the name, Maria Peixoto: some would surely have been expected from a man whose mistress—according to Mayhew—had been found in such a condition.

Was Millington a twister?

Halfhyde stared out ahead, his face set into hard lines. There was dishonesty about—either that, or a lack of trust. He disliked being used in such a way, hazarding his ship for a mission that even now was unclear. He cudgeled his brains: what could possibly be done to negate what was probably a perfectly legitimate agreement between two sovereign nations? Even intrigue could scarcely upset it now; and it could be presumed to be unlikely that Wainscott would be required to use his armed seamen in some ridiculous attempt to mount an attack on the base and either seize it or blow it up. The attempt alone would surely force the very war that the British Government clearly did not want.

There was a step on the ladder: Commander Wainscott. He approached the rail and stood alongside Halfhyde. He asked, 'Well? What did you think of him? As a man—you understand?'

Halfhyde voiced his thoughts. 'Unforthcoming. I'll now ask *you* a question, Commander: I gather Mayhew told him of the body.'

'Yes.'

'And of the supposed identity. Was there at that time any reaction to the name, Peixoto?'

'As a matter of fact, no, none at all that I could see.'

'In that case either we have the identity wrong—'

'Which is very possible.'

'Yes. Or Millington doesn't want any connection known. But it *is* known—to the Foreign Office as represented by Mayhew. Do I take it that Millington's not necessarily aware that his private life is known in Whitehall?'

'I think you may assume that until now, at any rate, he's had no suspicions, Halfhyde—'

'So he's not wholly trusted?'

Wainscott said, 'That's Mayhew's province. Not mine. I really can't comment.' He somewhat obviously changed the subject. 'The tide's running strongly, even so far up river as this. Shall we keep to our ETA, do you suppose?'

'So long as I can maintain my present speed, yes.'

Wainscott nodded but said no more. A few moments later he turned away and went below. Halfhyde, pacing the bridge, looked aft and saw him talking to Mayhew and Millington. There was a good deal of gesticulation from the Foreign Office man, who had the appearance of justifying himself in some argument. Soon after this the rain came back and the three men beat it fast for the door into the after alleyway.

iii

'It's very close, is it not?' Todhunter said. Night had come down and he had not been able to sleep: he ran with sweat so much that his bunk mattress soon became soaked and smelly. He had pulled on a dressing-gown and gone out on deck in his carpet slippers, the last present from his old mother. In the after well-deck he had found Petty Officer Parker, also unable to sleep but in his case on account of carnal desire; Victoria tended to flaunt her presence despite Halfhyde's strictures.

'Close and humid.'

'Very close and yumid, Mr Tod'unter.'

'Close in another sense too.'

'Eh?'

Todhunter waved an arm. 'The shore.'

'Aye. Shoals an' that.'

'Wild animals no doubt. And natives.'

Todhunter shivered, seeing himself, if Captain Halfhyde or Mr Briggs should err in their course, being torn to shreds by armadillos or spears wielded by men just as wild—dismembered like that poor body. 'Do you know these parts?'

Parker shook his head and spat a stream of tobacco juice over the bulwarks. 'Not me! Never bin down this way. Pompey, the straits, China, Singapore, all them places and a few more.' He gave the policeman a pitying glance. 'I s'pose you've never bin anywhere like that, eh?'

'Oh yes I have,' Todhunter said, his mind going back across the years to the days when he had been responsible for capturing the traitor Savory, which was something one could not discuss with a gunner's mate. 'South America—not up here, though—and south-west Africa—'

'That's wild enough.'

'Yes, to be sure it was. But there's a different feeling about the Amazon. I believe the natives are very quick to react against white men when they encounter them, and that they employ poisoned darts and such, in blow-pipes.'

'Aye, maybe they do, Mr Tod'unter, and you can't 'ear the buggers coming either. Plop—like that.' Petty Officer Parker gave the policeman a sudden dig in the ribs.

Todhunter cried out involuntarily. Angered,

he said, 'Kindly don't do that again. One does not wish to attract attention.'

'Sorry I'm sure, Mr Tod'unter.'

They stood there in silence, Todhunter feeling the weight of his woolly dressing-gown and wishing it were decent to take it off and take what air there was in his nightshirt; Petty Officer Parker darting discreet glances towards the master's deck and hoping the girl would feel the heat and come out into the open starkers, as he'd heard women sometimes did in the passenger liners in the Red Sea—there was a moon in the sky now the rain had once again cleared away and he would get a good view. But he had no luck: no one emerged from the cabin and Parker was left to speculate on what might be going on inside. He had a good imagination. So, for other matters, had Mr Todhunter. The shore was indeed very close at times, so close that it might not be too long a stretch of fancy to imagine the grotesque, hairy arms of apes and gorillas reaching out to seize him from the ship and convey him to some horrible lair in the forests and swamps. Mr Todhunter gave a sudden alarmed bleat as the *Taronga Park* came beneath the wispy overhang of a tree whose branches reached some distance from the shore.

Petty Officer Parker came back from his reverie. 'What's that, then?'

'Nothing really.'

'What you want to yell out for, for God's

sake?'

'I'm very sorry.'

Peelers! Parker grunted angrily. Flatfeet had no business aboard a ship. There had been any number of rumours as to what Todhunter was doing on the *Taronga Park* but no one seemed really to know. Barsett, the captain's steward and as such the usual avenue for information, either didn't know or wasn't saying, and that was funny in itself. Captain's stewards always had big ears to hang around conversations and were not above putting those ears to pantry bulkheads, and they usually liked the importance of being able to impart what they'd picked up on their antennae. Not this time, though. Petty Officer Parker was about to take a chance and ask the peeler straight off when Todhunter decided to go back to his bunk.

iv

A little after the *Taronga Park* had weighed anchor and moved out from the port of Gurupá, a Brazilian, moustached and sombreroed, had ridden out on horseback, making west through rough, inhospitable country for the township of Pôrto de Mos, where he delivered a message, which was at once taken on by another man, a German. He crossed the Xingú River in a boat and reached a village where he was provided with a horse that carried him to a settlement on the banks of the main river. From here he was

145

able to send a message by semaphore across the river to an outpost manned by German naval ratings. By means of the field telegraph line laid by the Germans the message reached the officer commanding the base on the Curua River: the British consul at Santarem had been in Gurupá to meet a steamer named *Taronga Park*, which was now proceeding up river with the consul embarked. No cargo had been discharged in Gurupá, and the sole purpose of the steamer's visit appeared to have been to embark the British consul.

v

'Santarem ahead, sir, round the next bend.'

'Thank you, Mr Briggs.' Halfhyde paced his bridge. In Santarem he would take the *Taronga Park* alongside the jetty, which, according to Millington, was a more solid construction than that at Gurupá. In the meantime, Millington had been a little more forthcoming insofar as he had informed Halfhyde that an official from the British Embassy in Rio de Janeiro was expected in Santarem and might well have arrived already. There would be discussions of what Millington referred to as 'ways and means'.

'I await the outcome,' Halfhyde said, 'with interest. And I suppose I am to take it I shall not be party to the discussions?'

'Not unless you are required to employ your ship as part of the—'

146

'Ways and means?'

'Precisely,' Millington answered. 'Our man in Rio will be accompanied by a high-ranking officer of the Brazilian Navy, representing the interests of his own country.'

'And the agreement with the German Emperor?'

'Naturally he will bear that in mind.'

It was more and more curious. Undoubtedly there was to be jiggery-pokery, else why not bring the Germans into the discussions? They presumably had an embassy in Rio de Janeiro. And it was odd, if diplomatic means were to be employed in an above-board fashion, that the German Navy on the Curuá River was not to know the true purpose of the *Taronga Park*'s presence on the Amazon. The developments, such as they were to date, were surprising to Halfhyde.

But there was a much bigger surprise waiting for him at Santarem.

vi

As they made their approach to the port, Millington was on the bridge with Wainscott and Halfhyde. There seemed to be something of a stir behind the jetty. The town, a larger one than Gurupá, had somehow the appearance of being *en fête*. There was a sound of music drifting across the scummy water, and crowds of natives were gathering.

'What is it?' Halfhyde asked.

'They're welcoming my return,' Millington said with an air of self-importance. 'Though I fancy it goes a little way beyond that. Indeed, I believe our guests from Rio de Janeiro have arrived ahead of me. Do you see?'

Halfhyde lifted his telescope again. Along the jetty, two men were proceeding—one tall, in plain clothes, a white suit and a topee, the other short and fat like Millington himself, legs twinkling in an effort to keep pace with the long strides of the tall one. The short man was evidently the high-ranking Brazilian naval officer referred to by Millington. He was in a garish uniform: white, with many brass buttons, large gold epaulettes with tassels, cocked hat and sword and, incongruously, white shorts so long and wide that they flapped about his knees as he walked. His face was beetroot red, again like Millington, and he wore a monocle that gleamed and sparkled in the bright sunshine, which had replaced the rain.

There was a similarity—not really to Millington, but ... Halfhyde checked his fancies. It was simply not possible. It couldn't be! It was sheer coincidence.

As the *Taronga Park*, proceeding at dead slow on the engine, came closer, Halfhyde began to believe he must be going mad. The strange figure in Brazilian uniform seemed to be a reincarnation of none other than his old

commanding officer and adversary, Captain
Watkiss of the Royal Navy, last seen sinking
into the blue waters of the Pacific Ocean some
years before.

CHAPTER TEN

The similarity, as the *Taronga Park* came
alongside and the two men waited for a
gangway to be rigged, was incredible. The long
shorts alone, a speciality of Captain Watkiss.
The monocle with its black silk cord, the
impatient, pompous manner, the shape, the
way he bounced on his feet. Memories
abounded of a capricious, autocratic, bombastic
post captain in command of a battleship, none
other than the old *Meridian* bound for South
America to be handed over in her obsolescence
to the Chilean Navy, carrying Detective
Inspector Todhunter to discharge his duty in
regard to the traitor Savory. Memories of
ludicrous orders, of swift changes of mind, of
an ability always to think himself in the right, of
a hidebound officer who, when in command of
one of Her Majesty's ships, considered himself
to be God's representative as well as Her
Majesty's. There had been much of the theory
of Divine Right about Captain Watkiss...

Halfhyde heard a sudden exclamation from

149

below the bridge and he looked down from the rail. It was Todhunter, full of amazement and a recognition similar to Halfhyde's.

Todhunter said, 'Well, I never did!' Looking up towards the bridge, he caught Halfhyde's eye. 'Do you see?'

'Yes, Mr Todhunter. But I think our eyes deceive us.'

'I'm not so sure, Captain Halfhyde, sir.'

Below on the jetty the Brazilian officer was showing signs of impatience at the delay in getting the gangway ashore, and talking meanwhile to the man from the embassy. He was also waving a telescope about in a dangerous fashion, another Watkiss attribute. Halfhyde, ringing off his engine and keeping an eye on the business of sending out lines to secure the ship to the jetty, was aware of Millington and Commander Wainscott leaving the bridge and going down to stand by the gangway as a committee of welcome to the Brazilian Navy. The moment the gangway was rigged the uniformed officer bounced aboard, followed by the civilian. Halfhyde heard a once familiar voice, loud and very British.

'Good morning. Who are you, pray?'

'Millington, sir, British consul here at—'

'Yes, yes, I see. I am Admiral Watkiss of the Brazilian Navy. Where is the ship's Master?'

'On the bridge, sir—'

'Indeed? I am accustomed to being met in

150

person by the captains of ships. What is the captain's name, may I ask?'

'Captain Halfhyde, sir.'

There was a pause. 'Did I hear you say *Halfhyde?*'

ii

'Dammit, man, you left me for dead!'

'I apologize, sir.'

'*Apologize?*' Admiral Watkiss brandished his telescope. 'I'll give you apologize, Mr Halfhyde, and damned if I'm going to call you captain! You—you—you should be in chains, charged with murder of your commanding officer—'

'You appeared to be sunk, sir. After you dived from the Japanese battleship a search was, of course, made, and—'

'Not a thorough one! I was alive, you fool! I was able to breathe although I had gone deep ... air had become trapped when my jacket went over my head, don't you damn well see!'

'But the rifles, sir—there was a body.'

'Oh, rubbish, it was a blasted Japanese corpse, a man who'd probably been unhandy enough to damn well fall overboard. They wouldn't have missed him till the next muster if then, I shouldn't wonder, the little buggers swarm like rabbits. However, as I was saying. When I surfaced at last, in some distress I may tell you, I found myself some way distant and was quite unable to make anyone hear. Such

151

damned insolence!' The telescope was waved again. 'I floated for some hours during which time you steamed away. At length I was picked up by some brave fellows in a fishing boat—Japanese, but brave nevertheless. More so than you, Mr Halfhyde. For a lieutenant in Her Majesty's fleet you were a damned disgrace!'

Halfhyde swallowed his anger. Regretful though he had been at the apparent death of the choleric Captain Watkiss, and tending to blame himself for the fact of Watkiss having been in danger from British small-arms fire directed at the Japanese, he felt no blame for leaving an apparently dead man to sink. Eyewitnesses had reported Watkiss unfortunately shot, and by that time there had been nothing visible. A longer search had been considered useless. There was now, however, no point in trying to justify himself in Watkiss' eyes.

Halfhyde said, 'May I congratulate you on your promotion, sir?'

Watkiss bounded up and down. 'Don't be impertinent, Mr Halfhyde. A dago navy—' He checked himself. 'Stout fellows all of them. I am appreciated, the more so as I have served Her Majesty, who is much admired in Brazil.'

'More than the German Emperor, sir?'

'What? Oh, I see you're about to split hairs again, Mr Halfhyde, as you always used to.' Watkiss, Halfhyde thought, was able as ever to turn a conversation against his listener. At this point Mayhew, who had joined the others at the gangway, intervened. He gave a cough, and Watkiss swung round.

'You're the man from the Foreign Office, am I right?'

'Er—yes, Admiral.' Mayhew coughed again. 'If I may suggest it, with respect, I think we should go into private conference rather than—'

'You do, do you?'

'Yes, Admiral, I—'

'Foreign Office! Bunch of pimply clerks! I always said so, did I not, Mr Halfhyde?' Watkiss gave a sudden chuckle and dug Halfhyde in the ribs with his telescope. 'Do you remember that dreadful fellow whatsisname aboard the *Meridian*, Mr Halfhyde?'

iii

'You'll have a drink, sir, for old times' sake?'

'I don't remember drinking with you before, a mere lieutenant. However, I shall do so. It's a hot day.' The conference was over; Millington had gone ashore to his residence and the man from the embassy remained closeted with Mayhew, Commander Wainscott and Detective Inspector Todhunter in the saloon. Admiral Watkiss had detached himself irritably, making reference to a blasted talking shop, and had come on deck for a breath of air. Halfhyde escorted him up to his cabin. At the sight of

153

Victoria, Watkiss stopped dead.

'Good God! A woman, Mr Halfhyde!'

'Yes, sir, a woman indeed.' Halfhyde made the introductions. Watkiss said disparagingly, 'Well, it's a merchant ship. What's her function aboard, may I ask? Stewardess, I presume?'

Victoria said, 'No, I'm bloody not! I'm a mate of the captain's'

Watkiss turned away. 'I detect an Australian accent, Mr Halfhyde—'

'Look,' Victoria said, moving forward. 'I'm here, so bloody talk to me and not bloody over me head, right? And don't you interfere,' she said, pushing at Halfhyde. 'I don't care who he is, but I'll tell you this, he's no more Brazilian than my left—'

'That'll do, Victoria.' Halfhyde's tone was peremptory. 'You'll kindly leave us. The Admiral and I have matters to discuss in private.'

She gave Halfhyde a withering look but left the cabin: she knew when not to argue. Admiral Watkiss placed his cocked hat on Halfhyde's desk, wiped his face with a vast red handkerchief, and sat down. 'A virago, Halfhyde.'

'With a heart of gold, sir.'

'Really. I believe they dig for gold in Australia, a dreadful country where the inhabitants show no respect for their betters and that's fact, I said it. However, there it is

154

and it's your own lookout. You spoke of a drink. I'll take whisky.'

'By all means, sir.' Halfhyde called for Barsett, and whisky was poured. 'Your very good health, sir.'

'Good God, you of all people, you may well say that with your tongue in your blasted cheek, Mr Halfhyde.' Watkiss drank. 'I suppose you feel entitled to know the facts of my rescue by those brave fellows. Or rather, what befell me later.'

'I would be obliged, sir.'

'Very well.' It was a long story as told by Admiral Watkiss but the bare essentials were in basis brief. The fishing boat had been overtaken by a typhoon after picking up Watkiss and had nearly foundered. They had survived because Watkiss had taken charge and shown the Japanese some British seamanship. Although he hadn't understood a word, he believed the Japanese to have been loud in his praise afterwards, even though their eventual landfall had been far from their homes—their instruments were primitive, their compasses pointing the wrong way, Watkiss believed—and they had ended up on the coast of South America.

'Peru, to be exact, Mr Halfhyde. The port of Máncora.'

'A long way, sir.'

'Yes, very. Short rations, Mr Halfhyde, and
155

we drank rainwater. We were driven by the winds. A feat of stamina on my part at any rate—those Japanase fishermen are used to it, doncher know. I believe I spoke of perseverance, a British attribute.'

'Yes, sir. And luck.'

Watkiss looked disagreeable. 'Oh, nonsense, it wasn't luck at all. However, we reached Peru and for a long time after that I was on the sick list. The strain, doncher know—I'm no longer a young man. I was looked after in the local hospital, a filthy place, but they pulled me through. I don't know what happened to the fishermen ... probably interned or something, being Japanese.'

'And you, sir? You were given your freedom?'

Admiral Watkiss screwed his monocle into his eye. 'I'm British, Halfhyde. I used my authority as a post captain in Her Majesty's fleet.' There was a pause, a long one, during which Watkiss looked somewhat shifty and embarrassed. Then he began a lengthy ramble concerning the naval attaché from the British Embassy in Rio de Janeiro, who after a great fuss had been made had crossed the frontier into Peru on Watkiss' behalf. He had brought unwelcome tidings from the Admiralty, in whose files Captain Watkiss had been written off dead.

'I said they'd better restore me at once, Mr

Halfhyde, since I was not dead, and find me a ship to command. But I was dissuaded from returning to England—certain factors emerged. There had been jealousy and I had been defamed. Had I lived when you left me for dead, it seems I would not have been re-employed. I believed I was too efficient for Their Lordships' liking. They saw their jobs in jeopardy I don't doubt, Mr Halfhyde.'

'Very possibly, sir.'

'Yes, I thought you'd agree. Anyway, to cut a long story short, the Brazilians were seeking an officer of experience to command their fleet, and I happened to be handy.'

'Unusual, sir, surely?'

Admiral Watkiss stared. 'What nonsense, my dear Halfhyde, it's not in the least unusual! Have you no regard for your naval history? Have you never heard of Admiral Lord Cochrane, Earl of Dundonald, a great seaman and officer? He accepted command of the Chilean Navy, did he not?'

'I understand so, sir. In 1818, having been dismissed from the British service after involvement in a swindle on the stock market—'

'Yes, yes, yes, and I call that downright disloyal, Mr Halfhyde, to drag that up. He served with great distinction in Chile and was much revered. However, as I was saying—with the help of our naval attaché in Rio I secured

157

the appointment. It seemed they particularly wanted a *British* officer, which is not in the least surprising, of course.' Watkiss sniffed. 'Damn dagoes! What a country! You can't expect foreigners to command fleets, after all.'

'But to them, sir, you yourself are surely a foreigner?'

'Oh, nonsense, of course I'm not! Being British ... it's very ubiquitous.'

'Quite so, sir. Very useful, I realize that.' Halfhyde paused. 'Your flagship, sir. Which is it?'

'Not a ship. Naval HQ ashore. Of course, I regret not being at sea.' Admiral Watkiss swatted at a fly that was buzzing about his ears. 'I ought to be grateful, certainly. But I find it pleasant to talk to a fellow British officer after all those dreadful Brazilians. And such decrepit ships, such appalling ships' companies with the officers all smelling of scent and looking like ponces in tight trousers! I am infuriated a hundred times a day, Mr Halfhyde,' he said pathetically. 'Often I yearn for the old days—clean paintwork, polished brass, smart sideboys at the quarterdeck ladder. Out here the sideboys appear to be born for one purpose only—buggery! They think nothing of it, I gather. I've tried to stamp it out but find no support from my—er.' Watkiss stopped and Halfhyde knew why: never would Watkiss refer to a foreigner as his superior. 'Mind you, I regard this conversation as being between you and me alone, Mr Halfhyde, never to be repeated. I am, after all, an admiral. I must show loyalty.'

'Yes, sir, I understand. But I think you're now faced with some difficulty, are you not? A dichotomy.'

Watkiss gaped. 'A dick what?'

'Dichotomy, sir. Split loyalties. Where, in fact, does the Queen stand now in your scale of loyalties?'

'In regard to the Germans' presence?'

'Yes, sir.'

'A fair question in the circumstances. The answer, of course, is that Her Majesty stands first. However, that's not something I wish to tell the dagoes. I am here in Santarem to help the British and the dagoes to an agreement of some kind in regard to the German base, Mr Halfhyde, and frankly I have to be seen to act in the dago interest. That's expected, naturally.'

'But you're not going to?'

'I prefer not to be too explicit,' Watkiss said angrily. 'That was always one of your damned faults, Mr Halfhyde, you are too forthcoming when what's needed is diplomacy.'

Halfhyde lifted an eyebrow. 'The forked tongue, sir?'

'There you go again! Balls and bang me arse, Mr Halfhyde, do you never learn?'

'I apologize. You are a loyal Brazilian, sir—'

159

'No I'm not!' Watkiss said energetically. 'But I must *appear* to be, don't you understand?'

'Perfectly, sir, perfectly. I shall be discreet, I promise you.' Halfhyde called for Barsett and more whisky. The glasses refilled he went on, 'This affair, sir, seems to be wholly in the hands of Mr Mayhew and the consul, plus Commander Wainscott who—'

'What about that policeman, whatsisname?'

'Todhunter.' Halfhyde shrugged. 'A mystery to me. He seems totally superfluous—'

'You don't know why he was sent?'

'No, sir. I wish I did.'

'H'm.' Watkiss pursed his lips. 'There is a possible reason, but one I can't discuss at this moment. You were saying?'

'I was about to say I've not so far been brought into the discussions. There seems to be a mistrust of seafarers.'

Watkiss bounced angrily. 'Typical! Blasted civilians, all wind and protocol, Foreign Office pimps who could do with being doubled round the fo'c'sle by a gunner's mate! If I had my way I'd string the buggers up to the gratings and give 'em a taste of the lash! They're always trying to hamstring men who get things done. The dagoes are just the blasted same and I find it most frustrating, Mr Halfhyde, most frustrating!'

'Yes, sir. Then ... can we not frustrate *them* for once?'

160

'How?'

'Can we not join forces, you and I, act in concert for Her Majesty? If you were to confide in me, sir, then something might be achieved. I can back myself to find some stratagem or other, I fancy.'

Watkiss stared through his monocle and rubbed at his chin with a hammy hand. He said, 'A stratagem. As I recall, Halfhyde, my dear fellow, you were always good at stratagems...'

iv

'I had a long talk with the Admiral, Commander. A useful one. To use my own phrase, not his, we are in cahoots. He's keen that you should join us; as a fellow naval officer he wishes you to share in certain facts, some of which may not be known to Mayhew and Millington.'

'Going behind their backs?'

'That can't be denied. But Admiral Watkiss has the Queen's interest at heart, and I know him to be extremely loyal.' Halfhyde gave Wainscott a summary of his own past service under Captain Watkiss' command and of the roundabout way in which Watkiss had reached South America and assumed the role of admiral in the Brazilian Navy. Wainscott knew not only about Lord Cochrane but knew also that historically a number of South American states,

161

who were accustomed to purchase worn-out warships from the British, had sought British officers to assume their highest naval ranks.

Halfhyde went on, 'Watkiss sees potential dangers in what is apparently a peaceful German trading base. In that, he is in accord with us—'

'How does he see the danger?'

Halfhyde shrugged. 'He's aware, of course, of the vulnerability of our trading routes in times of war—trade to South America and around Cape Horn to Australia or up the western seaboard to Chile and so on. He sees a threat to those routes, but that apart he was not precise. He is not a precise person, never was, but he is uneasy. And it's very much to the point that he wishes to frustrate any possible knavery on the part of the Brazilians, and that he wishes to act for the Queen.'

'Disloyal, surely?'

'To the Brazilians, yes. But Admiral Watkiss has never seen foreigners as *people*, Commander. Disloyal it may be, but who are we, loyal subjects of Queen Victoria, to refuse our co-operation in her interest?'

Wainscott nodded. 'You have a point. What does Watkiss propose?' He added, before Halfhyde could answer, 'Isn't there danger in it for Watkiss personally?'

'Yes, he realizes that, of course. He's not entirely disinterested as it happens. If he's seen to be of immense service to the Queen and the fleet ... you understand?'

Wainscott grinned. 'Back to the RN?'

'I believe he has that in mind.'

'A very long shot, bearing in mind what you've told me.'

'Admiral Watkiss has a skin like a rhinoceros, Commander. Everything bounces off, and he is able to convince himself that all's well, that basically he's held in the highest esteem—'

'You've encouraged him in this, Halfhyde?'

Halfhyde shook his head. 'Admiral Watkiss has never needed encouragement. In any case, I wouldn't mislead him. I've always had a certain regard for him. Apart from that, there's a degree of pathos ... so much bombast, most of it very transparent. I'd never knowingly let him down.'

'That speaks well for you.'

Halfhyde brushed that aside. 'By no means—I claim no credit for that. One can't help feeling immensely sorry, that's all. He's his own worst enemy. However, to return to what I was telling you earlier, Commander—'

'Certain facts, I think you said, not necessarily known to Mayhew and Millington?'

Halfhyde nodded. 'Or, I think, to you.' He paused. 'I told Admiral Watkiss about the body in the cable locker and that we believe it may be that of a Maria Peixoto. He understands from the gossip that she had indeed been Millington's

163

mistress.'

'Had been? Was the affair over, then?'

'According to Admiral Watkiss, it may be. She's known to have gone to England some months ago—Watkiss doesn't know for what purpose, nor who sent her, but he thinks it might have been her family, the family of Marshal Floriana Peixoto.'

'There's not much new in this, Halfhyde, is there? When Todhunter found that body, Mayhew told us what was known. I dare say the family *did* send her away, in order to protect their name. That would be natural enough, I'd say.'

'Yes. But that's not all, Commander. Admiral Watkiss believes that pressure is being put on Millington by the Peixoto family, who're immensely powerful—pressure to act against the British interest with regard to the German presence on the Curuá River.'

Wainscott looked startled. 'Great heavens, Halfhyde! What form does this pressure take, does Watkiss know?'

'He believes Millington may be under threat of assassination . . . we have to remember this is South America. Also that the Peixoto family is of course Catholic, and apparently very devout. It seems they have a relative who is a cardinal at the Vatican, and close personally to the Pope. They want no scandal. Myself, I don't find the threat in the least exaggerated, and Admiral

Watkiss appeared to know what he was talking about.'

'But from what you've told me of him ... is he not subject to flights of fancy, Halfhyde?'

'Well, he's not wholly reliable I have to admit. But I believe we must take this seriously insofar as we shouldn't put too much trust in Millington.'

'Perhaps. What is it the Peixoto family want of him?'

'In return for his safety ... he is to render false reports to London as to the German plans—'

'But look here, it was Millington's despatches that gave us the first warning!'

'Yes. That was before the affair with Maria Peixoto had become known. The moment the affair leaked, he was at risk. He had compromised himself, and could be made use of.'

Wainscott said, 'If all this holds water, then he'll be feeling himself in a pretty pickle now we've arrived!'

'Exactly, and Watkiss made that very point. His hypothesis is this: Millington was to report to London that there was no cause for worry after all, that he'd made an over-hasty first report, and all the Germans are doing is to assist the Brazilians with the loan of naval experts to oversee the construction of jetties and port installations for river-borne trade. For entirely

165

peaceful purposes, you see. Millington would guarantee to alert the home authorities immediately if the Germans should be seen to be making any kind of military preparation—but this, of course, he wouldn't in fact do.'

'Do I take it Millington has agreed to all this?'

'According to Admiral Watkiss, yes.'

'Why hasn't Watkiss reported it himself, to London?'

Halfhyde said, tongue in cheek, 'Admiral Watkiss is a Brazilian now, Commander.'

'Yes, but you said yourself his loyalties are to the Queen!'

'Indeed they are, but he must first look out for Number One. He has no wish to face a firing squad! Our arrival was fortuitous for him. From now on, he relies on us.'

Wainscott's face was grim. 'I never thought I'd see the day when a British consul could play the traitor. I'm not quite inclined to believe it now, in fact. Watkiss could be indulging in fantasies.' He paused, frowning. 'As to our own presence, won't we now be assumed to blow the gaff?'

'Only if Watkiss' revelations became known as having been passed to us. There is no reason why they should. I suggest we should play a waiting game, a game of cat and mouse perhaps, and keep a close eye on Millington.

'But if we're a threat to him and the Peixoto

166

family ... then are we not a target as well? Did Watkiss comment on that?'

'No. But I think we must regard ourselves as being at some risk. Accidents can happen in South American countries, and the truth need never emerge so long as a clean sweep is made.'

Wainscott was about to make a further remark when footsteps were heard on the Master's deck and a moment later Mayhew appeared in the cabin doorway.

'Ah—Wainscott. I fancied I should find you here. We have a visitor—two visitors. Captain von Grützner of the Imperial German Navy, and Senhor Arnaldo Peixoto.'

Halfhyde and Wainscott exchanged glances: it looked as if there might have been a leak already as to the true purpose of the *Taronga Park*'s visit to Santarem.

CHAPTER ELEVEN

Von Grützner, tall, elegant and black-bearded, was a man of excellent manners; and as a seaman he knew his priorities. The first heel-click, the first bow were for the Master; the second for Commander Wainscott.

'An honour to be allowed aboard your ship, Captain.' The English was perfect. 'I have much respect for the British sea services. You have, perhaps, sailed round Cape Horn?'

'I have, and under sail, Captain von Grützner.'

'Such splendid seamen!' The German turned courteously to Arnaldo Peixoto, who in Halfhyde's view resembled someone straight out of the days of the Portuguese royal house of Pedro I and the grandees of the olden times. He, too, was tall, with a commanding air—a handsome man with a thin moustache as black as the German's, and black, glittering eyes. There was a hint of sadism, a hint of the devil. Beneath the immaculate white sharkskin jacket was the bulge of a revolver holster. The German went on, 'Senhor Peixoto is a good friend of both our Emperor and your Queen.'

'A pleasure to hear that,' Halfhyde said. 'You are welcome aboard my ship, gentlemen.' Once again he called for his steward. Barsett appeared with a tray, bringing whisky and sherry. When the glasses were filled solemn toasts were drunk.

'To Her Majesty the Queen-Empress, grandmother of my Emperor. May she continue long upon her imperial throne.'

'To His Most Excellent Majesty the Emperor of Germany, grandson of Her Majesty Queen Victoria ... and to His Excellency Dr Manuel Ferraz de Campos Salles, President of the Republic of Brazil.'

There was a response to this by Senhor

Peixoto but as his peroration climaxed in a good deal of national emotion, there was an interruption.

ii

'You there, that policeman what's-your-name.'

Mr Todhunter, leaning over the after bulwarks for a breath of such air as might be found in this steamy land, swung round to find Admiral Watkiss flourishing his telescope from the top of the gangway.

'Todhunter, sir. Detective Inspector Todhunter of the—'

'Ah yes. Todhunter. You'll remember me from the battleship *Meridian*, no doubt.'

'Indeed I do, sir, indeed I do. You were then a captain in the British fleet, sir—'

'Yes, I know that, thank you, Todhunter. Now—a word in your ear.' Admiral Watkiss approached closer. 'I saw one of the da—Brazilians go aboard after I left, together with one of the Huns, so I've not got long—my presence will be required, obviously, and I'm damned if I know why I wasn't told the buggers were coming. However, that's not your concern, Todhunter—'

'No, sir, it—'

'Kindly hold your tongue and listen. I dislike being interrupted. I wish to know why you're here in Santarem, why you're aboard the *Taronga Park* at all.' Watkiss' own opinion was

169

that Todhunter had very probably been sent in case it became necessary to arrest the British consul, but he proposed not to make any direct mention of this currently. 'Frankly, I'm astonished that a London policeman should be found in Brazil, but no doubt there's some good reason—I'm not forgetting your arrest of the traitor Savory in Chile. Perhaps there is something similar this time, eh, Todhunter?'

'Oh, I don't think so, sir. Not a traitor, no.'

Admiral Watkiss stared at Todhunter, blue eyes bulging. Was he speaking the truth? Almost certainly not; policemen tended to conceal things, it was in their natures. 'Then what, may I ask, is your brief?'

Todhunter sucked in his cheeks, not liking to confess that he had no idea. That would appear amateurish and unworthy of the Force. He fell back upon his catch-all phrase: 'Why, sir, simply to uphold the law.'

'Balls,' Admiral Watkiss said impatiently. 'In Brazil?'

'Well, sir—'

'You're prevaricating, Todhunter.' Watkiss dug the detective inspector in the ribs with his telescope. 'I wish to know the facts, I'm blasted well entitled to in my position, and as I said, I'm in a hurry. Speak, man!'

Doggedly, a native London obstinacy coming to the fore, Todhunter shook his head. 'I'm really very sorry, sir, very sorry indeed, but I

170

have told you all I know, which I admit is not very much—'

'It certainly is not, a confession of total ignorance!'

'Yes, sir, and I repeat my apologies for the same. But even if I knew, sir, it would be most improper of me to inform you. My Chief Super—'

'Oh, blast your wretched superior, Todhunter, and I dislike stupid abbreviations such as Chief Super—that's all very well in the company of your equals but should not be used to me. You will kindly remember that I'm an admiral, Todhunter.'

'Yes, sir. That's the point, sir. With respect, of course,' Todhunter added politely.

Watkiss stamped his foot on the deck. 'What blasted point?'

'You're a Brazilian gentleman now, sir.'

Watkiss reddened dangerously. 'I am damn well not!'

'With respect again, sir, I'm forced to disagree. I really am, and I do apologize, but I cannot with a clear conscience reveal anything of what might or again might not be my orders from my—my Chief Superintendent, sir, to any foreign gentleman whatsoever, whether he be an admiral or whether he be not.'

Admiral Watkiss shook his telescope threateningly, his face mottled. 'You're a blasted idiot, Todhunter, and that's fact, I said it.' He seemed about to strike, but evidently thought better of it. He turned away and bounced for'ard towards the central superstructure. Mr Todhunter mopped at his face and found his hand shaking. Captain, now Admiral Watkiss was such a blooming tyrant ... it had been a very close shave indeed. He needed taking down a peg or two but Mr Todhunter's memory told him that Admiral Watkiss had always been absolutely immoveable on his exalted peg, which was firmly cemented in by his own self-estimation.

iii

'Good afternoon, Senhor Peixoto. I should have been informed that you were coming aboard.'

The Brazilian's thin lips parted in a smile, an oily one Watkiss thought. 'So that I could be received with my due honour, Admiral?'

Arnaldo Peixoto, Minister for Army and Marine, liked his honours; but such was not uppermost in Watkiss' mind. He said stiffly, 'That would have been accorded, naturally. But the point I'm making is that I should be present at any discussion between the Germans and my own—between the Germans and British representatives. That's my job as Commander-in-Chief of the fleet. Insofar as the state of readiness of the navy is concerned, doncher know.'

Peixoto showed his teeth again; they were

very white. 'My dear admiral, we do not propose to mobilize, we do not propose to go to war!'

'I didn't say we did. I spoke of readiness only, Senhor Peixoto.'

The Brazilian shrugged and said indifferently, 'It is of no consequence really. We speak only of friendliness between our country and Germany and Great Britain, three countries having most excellent relations. These we hope will continue. Is that not so, Senhor Mayhew?'

'Certainly, Senhor Peixoto. That is indeed the wish of my Queen.'

'Captain von Grützner.'

'Germany also.' Von Grützner clicked his heels and bowed. 'My Emperor is a reasonable and peaceful man—'

'What balls!' Watkiss said under his breath, but a little too loudly. Von Grützner lifted his eyebrows. Watkiss said hastily, 'Marble halls ... His Excellency is accustomed to live in marble halls which may on occasions distort his view of the relative ... of the lives of common people ... and then there's the Americans ...' He floundered, red-faced, to a stop. 'I'm sorry, Captain. Possibly I misheard your reference.'

'I accept your apology, Admiral.' Von Grützner inclined his head. 'But I think perhaps the fact of your British nationality renders you—'

'No, it doesn't! What nonsense! I am totally impartial.'

'But first for Brazil?' Peixoto broke in pointedly.

Watkiss set his teeth hard. 'Yes.'

'You think now as a Brazilian?'

'Yes.'

'You are committed, you feel yourself to be Brazilian?'

'Yes!'

'Then that is good. Let us continue the discussion.' Peixoto turned to Halfhyde. 'Captain, the reason for your coming to Santarem. You spoke of trade?'

Halfhyde nodded. 'I did, Senhor Peixoto. A cargo of manufactured goods from Birmingham.'

'Consigned to Senhor Millington, yes.' Peixoto gave his mendacious smile again. 'But I think we are all agreed this is a mere fiction, Captain?'

Halfhyde, knowing that this was Mayhew's province, delayed his answer.

The diplomat said smoothly, 'The cargo is under hatches, Senhor. That is no fiction, I promise you. The discharge will take place the moment the port's ready to receive it.'

'Yes. But the rest is fiction. The real reason lies elsewhere. How many of your merchant ships, Senhor Mayhew, are to be found with a high-ranking diplomat aboard, to say nothing of

174

a commander in your war fleet? How do you explain this, Senhor Mayhew?'

Admiral Watkiss showed restiveness as Mayhew shrugged: the wretched fellow, he saw, was undecided as to what to say next, though any diplomat worth his salt ought to have a string of lies at the tip of his tongue. There was some humming and ha-ing and then Mayhew gave his answer, an unsatisfactory one Watkiss thought: 'Oh, I'm here entirely incognito, so is Commander Wainscott—'

'Incognito? The word has a—'

'I amend the word,' Mayhew said hastily. 'I meant we're not here in any official capacity. Merely to observe.'

'Observe the base construction, Senhor?'

'It is of interest, certainly.'

'But of course!' Peixoto smiled again. 'That I understand. I am surprised only that you have not been honest, that you have tried to prevaricate. Of course your government is concerned at any development that involves the German Navy—that is natural, yes?'

'Yes,' Mayhew said, his face tight.

'Then now we all know where we stand, gentlemen.' Peixoto looked round the group. 'I, representing the Republic of Brazil, wish only the good of my country and an extension of its trade and its trading facilities. Captain von Grützner oversees the interests, again the trading interests, of his Emperor. And Her

175

Majesty Queen Victoria sends in a spy disguised as a diplomat, to find out whether or not the German Emperor intends warlike preparations. Is that not so, Senhor Mayhew?'

'Certainly not! I deprecate any suggestion of spying! To take an interest is not to spy, Senhor Peixoto.'

Peixoto gave an ironic bow. 'I apologize for the use of the word, Senhor Mayhew. Perhaps the seeking of information would be a better way of putting it. But I am not impressed with the action of your government in sending you to Santarem without any word of explanation or permission from my President.'

'I can't comment on that,' Mayhew said stiffly.

Peixoto laughed. 'Perhaps not.' He waved an arm, airily. 'Comment would be superfluous in any case. The matter is as I have stated it. And I shall show you that we Brazilians are above petty rivalries and disputes in the world beyond the seas where powerful nations fall out. You shall see what you regard as our secrets. Subject to the permission of Captain von Grützner you shall be received upon the Curuá River to inspect for yourselves, gentlemen. Captain von Grützner?'

'Of course, Senhor Peixoto.'

'Then it is agreed? Shall we say, the afternoon after tomorrow, by which time Senhor Millington will have arranged for the ship's cargo to be discharged?' There were nods from Mayhew and von Grützner; then Peixoto went on smoothly, the glitter in his eyes more pronounced than ever, 'In the meantime I must ask that none of the ship's crew or passengers go ashore. Is that understood?'

Mayhew looked astonished. 'But really—'

'I am sorry, it is to be considered an order. Admiral Watkiss?'

'Yes?' Watkiss snapped.

'There is no policeman in Santarem, Admiral. Therefore I ask that you provide a naval guard to ensure that my orders are obeyed.'

Admiral Watkiss placed his monocle in his eye. 'I must protest, Senhor—'

'I am sorry, that also is an order. You will remain yourself, and take up your quarters in the British consulate, where you will be comfortable enough. Your President relies upon you to act in the Brazilian interest. Well, that is all, gentlemen.'

Followed by von Grützner, Peixoto left the cabin and made his way down for the gangway.

iv

'Just look at that old bloke.' Victoria pointed towards the end of the jetty: Admiral Watkiss was to be seen sitting in a deck chair, his cocked hat on his head to ward off the sunlight, which was still strong even though the time was now

177

drawing towards dusk. On a table beside the Admiral stood his evening drink, a bottle of whisky and a soda siphon. He was looking much disgruntled, so much was plain even at a distance. 'Takes his job seriously, I reckon.'

'He explained before he went back ashore.'

'Explained what, mate?'

Halfhyde said briefly, 'No policeman. And no navy. Just him, until Peixoto sends reinforcements.'

Victoria's eyes widened. 'Poor old bloke, eh? Going to be there all bloody night, is he?'

'Probably.'

'He'll drop off soon, pissed on the whisky. Anyone who wants to get off the bloody ship—'

'I've foreseen that and I've given orders. Parker and his leading hand will watch the decks throughout the night.'

She gave him a look. 'Whose side are you on, then?'

'Ours. Trouble with the Brazilian authorities won't help, Victoria. And Watkiss . . . he was once my Captain. I have no intention of bringing him trouble.'

She jeered. 'Getting soft, aren't you?'

'Perhaps.'

'Well, you could be right, mate. Poor old bloke don't look up to it. Getting on, isn't he?'

'Yes. By now, he'd be retired from the British Navy unless he'd been promoted.' Halfhyde lifted his telescope and studied the

178

shore. Santarem was not much of a place, and its smell was strong—lack of drainage and sanitation, the odd straw-hatted native relieving himself in the street, carcases of mangy dogs lying in what was left of the sun, the Brazilians too lazy even to throw the corpses into the river. There were people around, drifting along, entering and leaving a shanty-like bar where the local liquor was on sale. Halfhyde watched the regular lift of a white-clad arm as Admiral Watkiss took his drink. From time to time a fly-swatter was lifted and brought into use, flailing about the Admiral's head as he tried to disperse insects that buzzed and bit. Just before the sun went down and obscured him from sight, a small procession was seen coming into view from behind the waterfront, approaching the jetty: the consulate servants bringing dinner for Admiral Watkiss on sentry-go. A table larger than the drinks one, a clean white cloth, cutlery, plates, and the meal itself in what looked like an empty whisky case. Halfhyde could only guess at what was being fed to Watkiss. A crowd that had gathered to watch disrespectfully had a better view until an angry shout from the Admiral dispersed them about their business.

Victoria giggled. 'Language, language,' she said. 'Talk about Australians! I reckon we've got nothing on the old bloke.'

'Kindly stop calling him the old bloke,

179

Victoria.'

'Temper!' she said, then snuggled against him as they stood by the guardrail. 'Sorry, mate. I reckon we're all at full stretch. What are we going to do, eh?'

'For the time being, masterly inactivity. We see what happens, Victoria, that's all.'

'Till after that Mayhew's been to the German place, d'you mean?'

He nodded. 'Probably.'

'What d'you reckon he'll see?'

'That's obvious: a trading base! By the time he gets there, the Germans'll have tidied up—shoved everything compromising well out of sight.'

'You reckon? Why didn't Mayhew think of that?'

Halfhyde sighed. 'I expect he did. But what could he say or do? Neither his edict nor Her Majesty's run in Brazil. We're all hamstrung, Victoria, caught in the web of diplomacy.'

'You'd better think something up, mate. You're the Captain.'

He gave a hollow laugh. 'Must I remind you again? This is Brazil. There have been three murders already—in Britain and aboard a British ship.'

'You mean—'

'I mean the Brazilians aren't much like Todhunter. They tend to shoot first, Victoria. We're all at risk now, if anyone puts a foot wrong. Poor Watkiss may be something of a comic turn. But the situation isn't.'

The dark came down, sudden as ever in the sub-tropical zones. There was a feel of coming rain again. Halfhyde was aware of the girl's shiver beside him. Below in the after well-deck a figure moved: Petty Officer Parker, carrying out the Master's orders, anonymous in no more than vest and pants but with a rifle and bayonet handily concealed in the lee of the after hatch. There was a sudden swirl of water and the snapping of great jaws as a big reptile made a meal of some passing carcase. Halfhyde looked down from the rail: in the light from a port he caught a glimpse of the beast as its tail disturbed the scummy water.

Victoria asked, 'What is it?'

'Alligator. *Jacare sclerops*. D'you see the ridge across its face? Fleshy eyelids ... it's often called the Spectacled Cayman because of its appearance.' Halfhyde paused, frowning. 'It's making upstream.'

'That significant, is it?' She sounded puzzled at his tone.

He shook his head. 'No. But it's given me an idea, Victoria.'

181

CHAPTER TWELVE

Masterly inactivity was all very well and had its undoubted uses, but Halfhyde had seen a possible opportunity and decided that the time had come for action.

He went down to the after well-deck.

'Petty Officer Parker?'

'Yessir!'

'I have a suggestion. For you, it's no more than that. I shall give no order. And this will be between the two of us, plus such of my officers and crew who'll need to know, do you understand?'

Parker said doubtfully, 'I don't know as I do, sir.'

'Then I'll be more explicit.' Halfhyde waved an arm towards the end of the jetty, where, by this time, a light had come on, a flickering lantern set on a pole, and was casting some luminosity over the occupant of the deck chair. 'Admiral Watkiss—he will soon, I fancy, fall asleep. In any case, he can't watch our starboard side.'

'No, sir.'

'I propose making my way upstream to the Curuá River, Parker, in the ship's lifeboat. The darkness is intense and will remain so, I believe. There'll not be any moon tonight—I expect rain, which will give good cover.'

'Aye, sir, that it will. You want me to go with you, sir?'

Halfhyde nodded. 'I'd appreciate it, Parker.'

'With Commander Wainscott's approval, sir?'

'No, I shall say nothing to the Commander, since if I did he'd be likely to forbid your leaving the ship. And I shall not ask you to go in your capacity as a naval petty officer.' Back in Liverpool, all the naval party had been officially signed on articles as supernumeraries, which made them, when it was expedient to cloak their Royal Naval status, into merchant seamen for the period of the voyage. 'What do you say?'

'I'll go, sir, and gladly—'

Halfhyde clasped his shoulder. 'Good man! Just the two of us, then—to see what we can find out before the Germans have had time to put a gloss on their base.'

'Yessir. Do we go armed, sir?'

'No. If we carried arms we might be tempted to use them, and then we'd end in some Brazilian gaol most likely. The idea will be to remain unseen. I—' Halfhyde turned as he heard a step on the deck behind him. There stood Detective Inspector Todhunter. 'Good evening, Mr Todhunter.'

'Good evening, Captain Halfhyde, sir.' Todhunter, hands behind his back, rocked on his heels, all at once very policemanlike. 'Without meaning any disrespect, sir. I happened to overhear what was being said.'

'Eavesdropping, Mr Todhunter?'

'Not eavesdropping, sir, no. Doing my duty, that's all, and sound carried like.'

'What, pray, do you propose doing about it, Mr Todhunter?'

'Well, sir, I have already debated within myself as you might say, me having been taught, in the words of my Chief Super, to think on my feet, and I have considered as to whether or not I should render a report to Mr Mayhew, sir, or Commander Wainscott, and—'

'Your decision, if you please, Mr Todhunter, and quickly.'

'Yes, sir.' Todhunter cleared his throat. 'As I say, I have considered. I found it no part of my duty to interfere with nautical matters, and this I consider to be a nautical matter since it involves the use of a boat. Further, it seems to me a wise move to take a look-see—in the circumstances that is, sir.'

'Yes, yes—'

'In which case it *does* appear part of my duties to accompany the mission, sir.'

'Ah. To uphold the law?'

'It may sound a bit silly, sir, in Brazil, but yes. That is what I am here for. That is, I think I am. To ensure that everything is done according to the law.'

184

Halfhyde grinned in the darkness. 'Did you see that passing cayman, Mr Todhunter?'

'Cayman, sir?'

'A species of alligator.'

'I failed to see it, sir, having only just come up on deck.'

'It was nasty, with immense jaws. There will be others out for food tonight. They move fast, like lightning, and snap viciously.' Halfhyde paused. 'Do you still wish to come, Mr Todhunter?'

Todhunter said, 'I never did *wish* to come, Captain Halfhyde. It's my duty, that's what. Frankly I shall be extremely, well, nervous. But the Metropolitan Police, sir, has a reputation to live up to, and my Chief Super—'

'Very well, Mr Todhunter, you shall come. But you'll be under my orders and you'll be as quiet as a mouse, and you'll assist by pulling on an oar.' Halfhyde added, 'We'll wait till close on midnight, till all's quiet ashore, and aboard too. Then I'll pass the word to the bosun to lower the lifeboat.'

ii

Mr Todhunter felt no qualms about pulling on an oar: he felt himself to be no mean rower. Many times in the past he had taken his old mother out upon the Serpentine in a rowing boat, his blue serge jacket off and his shirt-sleeves rolled up past the elbow and his bowler hat pulled down firmly in case it should be taken by the breeze to float at the end of its securing thread and make him the butt of small boys and their cruel laughter. He was well aware that the ship's lifeboat would be much heavier than the craft upon the Serpentine, but that would be, as it were, counterbalanced: his old mother had been heavy and unwieldy, pushing down the back end of the boat.

Halfhyde himself had been in a quandary: by his coming action he would be going against his own orders to Petty Officer Parker to ensure that none of the crew tried to outflank Admiral Watkiss. Now he was putting Watkiss at risk of censure for a poor watch if the lifeboat should be seen. Victoria had not been slow to seize on this.

'Doing the dirty on the old bloke—sorry, the bloody Admiral.'

'I know and I regret it. It's a case of one's primary duty. I think Admiral Watkiss would understand and applaud.'

'Buggered if I would if I was him. Not when I'd got the sack I wouldn't.'

'Admirals are never sacked, Victoria, they're put on the unemployed list. However, I see a way in which you can help.'

'Me?' she said suspiciously. 'How?'

'Provide him with an alibi. Something the Brazilians would find understandable, and forgivable even. They're a hot-blooded race—'

'Look, mate. What are you suggesting?'

He grinned down at her. 'Exactly what you're thinking: go and exert your charms.'

'Never! The old bloke's got no time for me, mate. You know that.'

'I also know Admiral Watkiss. He's been a lecher in his time and a pound to a penny he'll respond to a pretty face and a little flattery!'

'Yes, well. What if he responds too bloody far, eh?'

'He won't. He's an old man now. Besides, the lantern will remain lit and he'll not attempt anything beneath its beams.'

She said angrily, 'I never bloody agreed to go—'

'No, but you will, Victoria. It'll be an enormous help—England'll be eternally grateful—'

'Tripe!'

Halfhyde shrugged. 'All right, forget patriotism and do it for me. And Watkiss himself. Though if anything goes wrong the blame will fall on me, not him.'

She asked, what about her. He promised she would be protected. A woman would never be left in the lurch by the British Government or its representatives on the spot, and in any case the Brazilians were always gallant where the female sex was concerned. After further persuasion she agreed; and Halfhyde had quiet words with the First Mate in whose charge he

187

would leave the *Taronga Park*, and with the bosun. As midnight approached and everything had for some while been silent along the shore, and Wainscott and Mayhew had turned into their bunks, Halfhyde mustered in the fore well-deck with Petty Officer Parker and Mr Todhunter, the latter dressed in his blue serge jacket atop a pair of white duck trousers found him by the bosun, and wearing his bowler hat like a badge of office. The night was hot and humid and Todhunter looked uncomfortable, sweat melting the starch of his high white collar. The expected rain had not yet come, but, as Halfhyde had predicted, there was no moon; it lay totally obscured behind heavy cloud. So far, luck was with them. At the inshore end of the jetty the lantern glowed, casting light on Admiral Watkiss, his head slumped sideways in his deck chair. From the starboard side of the *Taronga Park* the lifeboat was swung out on the davits and the three men embarked, Todhunter very gingerly, from the bulwarks.

Under the quiet orders of the bosun the lowerers paid out the falls and the boat took the water with a gentle plop and a subdued rattle of oars and crutches. From his position as coxswain in the sternsheets, Halfhyde passed the next orders in a whisper.

'Bear off fore and aft ... give way together! No splashes, if you please, Mr Todhunter. And

188

catch no crabs.'

iii

At the German base the officers and senior ratings had been warned by Captain von Grützner that an official of the British Foreign Office would be arriving in forty-eight hours' time to see for himself that their intentions were purely peaceful. To this end they would next day remove all traces of anything that could be considered warlike. All cases, all items of naval equipment bearing the mark of the German Admiralty were to be stowed well away out of sight, as, of course, would be the defensive guns, the artillery pieces supplied by the Brazilians themselves, and all small-arms. All sentries would be withdrawn, and all ratings of the working-parties, when the British came, would be dressed, not in uniform overalls, but in a variety of gear to be provided by the native Brazilians who formed the labour force.

All that was for the next day. In the meantime the sentries were mounted as usual, and as usual they mostly slept handy for their posts: in friendly Brazil, there was little to guard against other than the odd thief in the night, and such marauders had dwindled rapidly after some had been caught and summarily punished by Captain von Grützner with the application of the cat-o'-nine tails wielded by a muscular member of the naval

189

police, before being handed over to the Brazilian authorities to face long terms of imprisonment. Even tonight, with the British close by in Santarem, there was a good deal of inertia: the British had been confined aboard their ship by orders of the Minister of Army and Marine and there they would remain. The British, it was well known, were hidebound, unimaginative, always very correct in their dealings with foreign governments and would not transgress any local laws and edicts. The spirit of Lord Nelson, it was said, no longer pervaded the British Fleet except on Trafalgar Day.

So the guard, feeling secure, was slack. One of the sentries, a seaman named Kurt Schmidt, marched his post for a while and then sat down beneath a tree to smoke his pipe, his rifle and bayonet propped against the trunk where a low branch grew to hold it. He puffed contentedly and listened to the waters of the river flowing down to meet the great Amazon that, when war came with the British, as come it would one day, would be filled with *Unterzeebooten* making out to sea to sink British shipping or returning from their glorious voyages to enjoy the pleasures of the land. It was whispered, and very possibly with truth, that Kaiser Wilhelm, wishful to keep his sailors happy and fulfilled, intended making arrangements for the export from Germany of the ladies of the

190

seaports—Wilhelmshaven, Bremen, Cuxhaven, Kiel, Hamburg—to the Curuá River. Kurt Schmidt greatly looked forward to this; the local women were not always easily come by and shore leave was not generous in any case. To have them on the spot would be truly a bonus. Schmidt pondered on certain things as he puffed at his pipe and occasionally drew a watch from his pocket to keep a check on the time when the Petty Officer of the Guard, a man of regular habits, would make his rounds. After a while nature called: Schmidt lumbered to his feet and approached the bank of the river for a pee.

With the recent rain, the bank was muddy and slippery. Schmidt lost his footing and slid towards the water, cursing. He went over the edge, willy nilly, to become submerged with his mouth filled with water and mud. By the time he heard the swish of a mighty armoured tail and saw the open jaws making for him at high speed, it was too late. Too late even to cry out.

iv

'Easy, Mr Todhunter, easy!'

Todhunter gave a gasp: he was nearly at the end of his tether. Dear me, he thought in anguish, it's a much longer way than I imagined. Nothing like the Serpentine either. His oar, a terribly long and heavy one, kept on missing the water—catching a crab in defiance of Captain Halfhyde's order—with the result that his desperate pull met no resistance and he collapsed backwards, again and again, falling against the next thwart with a bone-shaking crump that might lead to back trouble in the future. But he gritted his teeth and went on manfully with his task, from which there was no respite at all. Captain Halfhyde had said he didn't want to be all night over his mission; and he was turning into a slave-driver, worse indeed than the most pernickety chief superintendents to be found at Scotland Yard, and that was saying something.

Todhunter complained of a stitch.

'I'm sorry, Mr Todhunter, but it must be borne stoically.'

'It's almost like a hernia, Captain Halfhyde, sir.'

'Then you should have brought your truss, to be on the safe side.'

His truss! Todhunter, breathless from his exertions in any case, found no words in response, but he grew angry: Captain Halfhyde was making game of him. There had been a snigger from Petty Officer Parker. Todhunter pulled on, staring into pitch darkness, straining his back with every movement of his arms, which themselves had a most dreadful ache all the way along. A moment later the rain started. A terrible downpour, straight down into the boat from the sky, like all the inhabitants of heaven relieving themselves simultaneously and with malice aforethought. The rain bit and stung and drenched, even roughening the water alongside the boat. The boat itself began to fill. Mr Todhunter drew Halfhyde's attention to this in an alarmed voice.

'We shall be all right, Mr Todhunter, never fear.'

'But it'll rise, Captain Halfhyde—'

'If it does, you may use the baler as a relief from the oar, Mr Todhunter.'

'Thank you, sir. Relief would be the word!'

They slipped through the water beneath the pounding of the cloudburst, smelling vile smells as, perhaps, the drenching rain washed nasty things, dead things, from the banks into the river, things that from time to time smote heavily against the blade of Mr Todhunter's oar and jarred him viciously. He wished he'd not worn a starched collar: it was a soggy band around his neck. He pulled on: he must never let the Force down, and to be sure this would be a tale to tell when he returned to Scotland Yard. If ever he did. Mr Todhunter was virtually certain that he was the only detective inspector of the Metropolitan Police who had ever pulled a lifeboat up the Amazon in an expedition against the German Emperor. He was assuaging his mind with thoughts of the esteem in which his fellow policemen would hold him in the future when there was a sudden exclamation from Halfhyde.

'Poor fellow!'

At first Mr Todhunter thought Halfhyde was addressing him. Then he saw what Halfhyde had seen: passing the boat and coming from behind Todhunter from the direction of the German base was what he took to be an alligator, an immense beast with a rocky head and very long jaws filled with huge teeth biting into a human body that had ceased to struggle. From one side of the mouth as the beast flailed itself downstream by its tail protruded a head and chest; from the other a pair of seaboots. As the terrible sight moved past, very close to the boat, and vanished astern, Mr Todhunter could have sworn he heard a crunch.

Then Halfhyde spoke again. 'Almost there. I'll steer for the bank. From there we proceed on foot.'

CHAPTER THIRTEEN

Victoria studied her reflection in the looking-glass. She was a real treat, she thought with some satisfaction, enough to give the old bloke something he hadn't had for years—tight waist that showed off hips and bosom, a big hat with flowers on it like a garden, which she'd bought in Liverpool, hair neatly coiled beneath

194

it. She didn't look quite herself but she reckoned she looked a smasher all the same. To top it all off she had been generous with a somewhat obtrusive scent from a bottle acquired from the street market in London's Portobello Road.

She left the cabin and went down to the well-deck and the gangway to the shore. One of Petty Officer Parker's men emerged from the entry to the fo'c'sle. Victoria said, 'Captain's orders.'

The man touched his forehead. 'That's all right, missus.' Victoria gave him a gracious smile, lifted her skirt, and climbed onto the gangway. She walked along the jetty, skirt swinging seductively. She could see Admiral Watkiss and she could see that he was sound asleep and probably a bit tight. It was a shame to wake the old bloke and, she thought, bloody pointless really. If he was alseep he wouldn't see anything in any case, would never know what was going on during his sentry-go. But of course that wasn't quite the point, as Halfhyde had stressed. The point was the alibi; she walked on. It was a hell of a hot night, she thought, all sticky. Sweat started beneath her chemise and petticoat and stays and as she moved she could hear the creak of whalebone and feel it prod into her flesh. She sailed on mutinously, feeling like that Princess Alexandra who had married the Prince of Wales and was said to have much to put up with, what with all his flirtations and worse.

Men!

She reached Admiral Watkiss and stopped, wondering how best to wake him. A cough, a prod, a shaken shoulder, or a direct address loudly given?

She need not have worried: something, some sixth sense perhaps, had woken Watkiss. An eye opened, then another, and the old bloke sat as upright as the deck chair would allow.

He sniffed the air. 'What in God's name is that?'

'Me,' Victoria said. She saw him sniff again. 'And me scent. Don't you like it, then?'

'Filth. What the devil are you doing here, young woman, may I ask?'

'Come to see you. You looked lonesome, out here.'

Watkiss got to his feet with difficulty, still sleepy. 'You've no right ashore—have you come from the *Taronga Park*? I don't believe I've seen you before—how many blasted women does Halfhyde keep aboard?'

'You've seen me,' she said. 'It's just that I look different. Dressed meself up for you, see.'

'You're that woman?'

'I reckon so.'

'What's the blasted idea, damn you!'

'Like I said. Keep you company.'

'Really.' Admiral Watkiss fished up his

196

monocle and thrust it into his eye. 'What confounded impertinence! I know women of your sort! I'm fully aware of your blasted wiles! You'll get nowhere with me, young woman, nowhere at all. If you believe I can be suborned from my duty by that appalling stench and by a blasted hat more suited to a—a garden party at Buckingham Palace than a jetty in Santarem in the middle of the blasted night, then you'll believe anything!' He bent and picked up his telescope as if it were a defensive weapon.

Tears of anger and humiliation came to Victoria's eyes. She spoke shrilly; she had been much hurt. 'Sod *you* for a start, mate! Daft old bugger! Look like something out of the music halls with that bloody silly uniform, and talk about hats! Think you're Lord Nelson, do you, eh, cocked bloody hat and feathers out of a bloody bird's bum! I bet you're not capable of anything anyway, and you can guess what I bloody mean and then stick it up your arse!'

'Such language,' Watkiss said disdainfully. He waved his telescope. 'Be off with you! Be off with you this instant!'

'Don't you bloody worry, mate, I'm going all right.'

She turned away and went along the jetty as rapidly as her skirt allowed. She heard the shouted word 'Scum' floating on the air behind her. Her face flaming, cursing Halfhyde under her breath, she reached the gangway. The naval

197

rating was waiting at the top.

'All right, missus?'

'Shut bloody up.'

The seaman scratched his head as she made fast for the ladder to the Master's cabin. He'd heard it said that Australians were weird.

ii

'Take it as fast as you can,' Halfhyde ordered, 'whilst keeping as quiet as possible. We must keep a lookout for sentries. What is it, Mr Todhunter?'

'The mud, Captain—'

'It'll impede us I know, but it can't be helped.' The mud was terrible, and they sogged along with squelches and foul gas rising with each footstep. 'Lift your feet high.'

'It's not just the mud, sir. It contains what I believe are leeches.'

'No doubt after a meal of blood. Pull them off.'

'I—I can't, Captain Halfhyde.' Mr Todhunter was forced to use the word can't even though he had learned from his Chief Super that no less a person than Napoleon Bonaparte had said there was no such word; it was physically impossible to detach the horrid, slimy things from his legs, up the bare flesh of which they had crawled since the duck trousers, wide and baggy, had been forced upwards by the mud, and from his arms as he used them to

198

try to keep his balance and plunged them into the mud in so doing. 'They are having an effect upon me I do declare. I've never been able to abide snails even.'

'Kindly keep silent, Mr Todhunter.' Halfhyde's tone was a warning; Todhunter obeyed what was implicit in it, and forced himself through the dreadful morass, expecting at any moment to sink for ever into a swamp and find his mouth filled with leeches. There might even be worse denizens: he believed some appalling species of snake dwelt in mud and he quaked in fresh terror, wishing he'd never come. He might even meet an alligator for all he knew—they didn't always keep to the water, and the sight of that human body impaled on the teeth was very recent and would never fade entirely from his memory. Meanwhile the rain was continuing, seemed almost a solid curtain by this time, so fierce that it washed Mr Todhunter's top half more or less clean as the bottom half grew muddier and muddier. It was as though the world had very unkindly turned to water and mud. Mr Todhunter felt the beat of his heart, increasing in response to exertion and mounting fear of the unknown and the horrid. It thudded like a drum. Or a tom-tom? No, tom-toms were African, Mr Todhunter reminded himself. But South America held other things and among them were the blow-pipes filled with poisoned darts. But surely, on a night like this, not even a native would be abroad? They were very likely quite alone except for the sub-human things that dwelt in mud.

Behind Todhunter, Halfhyde said suddenly, 'A light ahead. A lantern. Do you see it, Parker?'

'Aye, I do, sir,' Parker said after a moment.

'That'll be the base. And a pound to a penny all the sentries will be under cover.'

'So long as the rain lasts, sir.'

'It has a lasting feel. It'll still be with us long after dawn, I fancy.' They moved on, the lantern their lode star as it twinkled and guttered through the otherwise pitch-black night. At one stage Mr Todhunter fell, and had to be extracted from the mud, having gathered more leeches; but soon after this they reached firmer ground and the progress became a little easier. Halfhyde called a halt near the lonely trunk of a solitary, skeleton-like tree.

He said, 'I believe we've reached a perimeter of sorts, though it's hard enough to perceive anything for certain. Mr Todhunter, I believe you are not happy.'

'No, Captain Halfhyde, sir, I am not.'

'Then I suggest you remain where you are, by this tree, while Petty Officer Parker and I go on—'

'I have my duty, sir—'

'I think you can feel satisfaction in that

you've done it, Mr Todhunter.'

'Do you really think so, sir?'

'Yes, I do,' Halfhyde said firmly.

'But if you go on, sir, and move out of my sight, then I shall be failing in my duty to watch and observe and—'

'No, you'll not, I assure you. We'll not be long—a quick reconnaissance and we return. There will be no contact with the Germans, and nothing at all that will call for your personal attendance, Mr Todhunter. And spare no thoughts for your Chief Superintendent—he's not here, and will learn only what is reported to him later. My report will be that you're a credit to the Force.'

'Very kind indeed of you, Captain Halfhyde, I'm sure—'

'Without you we would never have arrived—you pulled splendidly on your oar, and will pull as manfully on the return journey. Now we shall leave you.'

'But really, I—'

'No argument, Mr Todhunter. And just one order: don't move a step. You're on reasonably firm ground here, and quite safe.' Halfhyde and Parker moved away and were soon lost to sight in the teeming downpour. Todhunter quaked in his loneliness; quite safe indeed! Leeches, snakes, alligators, Germans. At any moment something like an armadillo might lumber along, and how did you combat armadillos?

They were, Mr Todhunter believed, armoured with thick, leathery hide, hence possibly their name. Safe be blowed! He was in immense danger and Captain Halfhyde didn't care a rap. Indeed, Mr Todhunter believed Captain Halfhyde had been mendacious, not concerned about safety but only with getting away with something beyond the law—either that or he felt that he, Todhunter, might be an encumbrance, someone who might fall flat on his face again at an inopportune moment and attract German attention.

There was a sound beside him: he almost jumped a mile. Goodness gracious! A rattle, yet not quite that. *A rattlesnake?* Sweat broke out. Mr Todhunter prayed, and the prayer was swiftly answered: remembrance came that rattlesnakes didn't live in mud and swamps. They preferred the dryness and the sun and the eating of little mice and birds. Now the rattle was more like a croak, as of some enormous toad or frog. Mr Todhunter felt his stomach lurch and his bowels loosen. The croak was coming from his left and seemed to be growing louder, and he moved away rapidly to his right. Something slithered across his foot and he gave a short cry of terror and moved faster, his feet splodging and making sucking sounds in his haste to get away from rattles, croaks and slithers. He wished desperately that he was back on the beat—anything, a mere constable in uniform—walking the Ratcliffe Highway and dealing with nothing worse than drunken sailormen and fallen women seeking to rob them of their money, carried in belts around their waists.

Then he lost the light.

'Oh, dear me!' he said aloud. What had happened? Had the rain doused the lantern, had something gone wrong for Captain Halfhyde, had the Germans been alerted?

Or was he simply lost? He had disobeyed orders when he moved from his spot. He would never find it again, never, not in this darkness, which lay like a blanket. What dreadful places there were in the world! Mr Todhunter moved this way and that, a few short paces here, a few short paces there, and then began to panic. He heard, or anyway thought he heard, the croaks and slithers again, and then a terrifying sound like something swishing the air, something that could easily be an alligator's tail but wasn't. He realized this when, after the swish had followed him for some distance and he was moving rapidly away towards he knew not where, the sounds altered and became human, the drag of feet through mud.

Oh, what a relief!

Captain Halfhyde, back much sooner than expected, and his ordeal was nearly over. It was a truism that the return journey was always much faster than the outward one and in any case it would be downstream.

Mr Todhunter stopped and turned round, ready to utter his relief. So thick was the darkness that he was almost crashed into, and then he felt hot breath fan his face and he smelled smoky-flavoured sausage and an angry, guttural voice spoke in an unknown tongue, unknown but in the circumstances guessable at.

iii

'Todhunter?'

Halfhyde was keeping his voice low; Petty Officer Parker was quartering the ground, carefully. There was no response to Halfhyde's soft call. He let out a long breath of annoyance. Up to this point his reconnaissance had been wholly successful and he had seen a great deal that was of immediate interest and he wished to make all speed back to the ship to report the German chicanery to Wainscott and Mayhew. And now Todhunter had vanished and thrown a heavy spanner into the works. Halfhyde, beneath his breath, cursed all meddling detective inspectors, but recognized his own culpability in agreeing to let the man come with him. It was in his view unlikely that Todhunter had been apprehended by any human, German, agency; the base had been wide open to the rain, not a man in sight anywhere, just as he had anticipated.

Parker approached. 'Not a sign, sir. And I

don't reckon we're adrift on our bearings either, sir.'

'No.' Todhunter's tree had been the only one so far as could be seen. 'And this is where the mud starts—I can hear the river, too.'

'Aye, sir. What do we do, sir?'

'Find the boat and make back aboard,' Halfhyde said. It was all they could do; the report was vital and Todhunter could be anywhere, in the stomach of an alligator or fallen victim to swampy ground, real swamp that might lie anywhere to suck a man down to a suffocating death. It was hard, but there was no alternative, and the one hope was to get back aboard and then, after daylight, mount a full search party with prepared excuses if they were seen by the Germans. Already time had been lost in the fruitless night search. There was probably no hope for Todhunter in any case. Both swamps and alligators were fast. The loss was going to be hard to explain, since Halfhyde had left the ship in defiance of Brazilian orders and without informing the representative of the Foreign Office. Possibly Admiral Watkiss could pour oil on troubled waters; but Halfhyde knew this was unlikely. The effect of Watkiss in the past had been invariably inflammatory.

With Petty Officer Parker, Halfhyde plunged again through the mud towards the river. In the faint sheen of light always to be found upon water in the darkest night, they picked up the

205

lifeboat without too much difficulty and drifted fast downstream on the current.

iv

A quaking bundle of sodden flesh, Mr Todhunter was marched ahead of a bayonet into the German base, where in fact the lantern was lit still, swinging from a pole outside a corrugated-iron-roofed hut. Here he was halted. Mr Todhunter believed he had lost the light when other buildings came between it and his line of vision as he had plunged about in despair, for now he could see a number of huts similar to the one he had been halted at, some bigger, some smaller.

The man said something in German.

'I beg your pardon,' Mr Todhunter said politely. Germans were Germans, of course, but should not be looked upon as the enemy since there was no war, and politeness cost nothing, as his old mother used to say. 'I don't—'

There was a push in his back, a hard one, and he lurched and stumbled about, falling against the door of the hut. 'Well, really!' he said breathlessly.

There was an impatient sound and the man reached past him and pushed the door open, then pushed Mr Todhunter inside. At a desk sat another German, in naval uniform with a peaked cap resting on the desk. He was a roughish-looking man, probably an NCO. He

206

stared at Todhunter in astonishment and there was some dialogue between the two men, but nothing emerged in English. After a lot of what Todhunter considered gabble, he was subjected to a search and then the first man left the hut and the seated one produced a revolver which he pointed at Todhunter and said something further, which Todhunter took to be a threat. He licked his lips but made no response.

After a long wait the man came back with another man, an imperious-looking man who was obviously an officer, though Todhunter was unable to see his uniform since he was wearing an oilskin that glistened with rain. The cap, however, bore a splendid badge of gold, while the face bore a neat beard similar to that of the German Emperor. There was more talk in German and then the officer raked Mr Todhunter from head to foot with eyes that seemed to pierce like red-hot pokers.

After a moment he spoke. 'You are who?'

English! Mr Todhunter was much relieved but at the same time worried: if they knew he was English, then they would at once connect him with the *Taronga Park* unless he was extremely careful, but of course he couldn't get away with trying to make out he was of any other nationality since he couldn't speak any other languages. Also, there was the bowler hat, still miraculously attached to its cord. Well, it was always best to come clean; honesty, to a policeman, was decidedly the best policy. He needn't be clean all the way, however. He knew his duty as a detective.

He said, 'Todhunter, sir.'

'Tod-hunter?'

'That's right, sir, yes, detective inspector from the Metropolitan Police. Scotland Yard, that is.'

The eyes snapped at him. 'I think you play the fool!'

'No, sir, indeed I don't.' For a moment Todhunter wondered if after all he'd played the wrong card: his jacket contained no identification, all his official documents were in his Gladstone bag aboard the *Taronga Park* and in fact he could have said he was anyone—if only he'd been confident of getting away with a false identity, which he hadn't been at all. But if they were not going to believe him anyway, and he could appreciate their difficulty, then he might just as well have tried to make out he was anybody, a professor from London University, for instance, searching for species of wildlife along the river bank. 'I'm what I say I am, sir, I do assure you, and I would like to be released if you don't mind.'

'First you will answer questions, Herr Todhunter.'

'I shall do my best, sir—'

'First, then. What are you doing here?'

'I'm afraid I can't answer that, sir, I'm sorry.'

Mr Todhunter was still very damp; rainwater trickled down his walrus moustache and he lifted a hand to brush it away. The German jumped backwards as though a gun was being drawn on him, and Todhunter apologized again. 'I have no evil intent, sir, none at all.'

'You have come from the British ship in Santarem—this is obvious—'

'Oh no, sir, no.' It was after all surprising how easy lies came, and an idea had presented itself to Mr Todhunter. 'Not a ship, sir, no. The British consulate, to—to which I've been attached, see?'

The disbelief was plain. 'For what purpose, Herr Todhunter?'

'On duty for Scotland Yard, sir. To—to make an arrest. There are certain extradition proceedings, sir, that require my presence—'

'In Santarem, perhaps. Not here, I think.'

'Ah,' Mr Todhunter said. 'Yes. Now, that *is* a different story I agree, sir.'

'Then please tell me that story.'

'Well, I don't know as how I can, sir. My Chief Super ...' It was always best to show reluctance initially and while you were showing it you could think. Criminals had often tried that on Todhunter but he'd always been too fly for them. He would have to be pretty astute now, to fool the Germans, but he had the advantage of being a detective inspector of much experience. 'I have my duty, sir, as you'll

209

appreciate, of course. I cannot break a confidence.'

The eyes glittered even more and the teeth showed, both metaphorically and actually. 'If you do not, Herr Todhunter, I may be forced to remove the velvet glove. Do you understand?'

'I think I do, sir, yes. But I have the protection of the British consul, representing Her Majestry, or rather Her Majesty's *Government*,' Mr Todhunter amended, preferring always to present the facts accurately. 'So you see—'

'No, I do not see anything. You have a British saying—possession is nine-tenths of the law—'

'Oh yes, sir, that's very true, but—'

'Very true, Herr Todhunter. We possess *you*. Much can happen that can be denied to your British consul afterwards. By treaty with the Brazilian Government, you are now upon German sovereign territory, Herr Todhunter.'

Mr Todhunter tried to outstare the piercing eyes but failed. His heart thumped painfully. He had heard a lot about the Germans and he knew a thing or two about how men could be beaten and yet not show any marks. Also, it wasn't entirely unlikely that he could be spirited away to Germany itself, a nasty overland journey, perhaps, though he couldn't see what use he could be in Berlin, so possibly he was over dramatizing his situation. He'd intended giving the officer a false reason for his presence but the difficulty was, he couldn't think of one, so, short of telling the truth and being in dereliction of his duty, he looked like being in for a rotten time of it.

v

'You're sure of your facts, Halfhyde?' Commander Wainscott, roused from his bunk, looked worried. He had never in fact been in doubt that the Germans were up to no good vis-à-vis the British interest, but now Halfhyde appeared to believe he had the positive confirmation; if he was right, then someone would have to act on it.

Halfhyde said, 'I believe it's beyond doubt now. It's all well disguised, but I can smell it out. It hasn't the feel of a trading base—much more that of a potentially defensible dockyard. No gun emplacements that I could identify as such, but sites being prepared I fancy. A number of huts that have a barrack look about them.' He paused. 'Pens that could be used for submarines—'

'*Submarines*? On the Amazon? That's sheer lunacy—'

'Wait a moment, Commander. I'm convinced the intention's for underwater craft—and I believe some of the crews may already have been drafted as an advance party. I picked up a German pay book as I take it to be. Here it is.'

He handed it over. It was rain-soaked and muddy, and folded as though it had been kept in the inadequate pocket of the German equivalent of a British bluejacket's rig. Wainscott opened it; he had no German but one word was easily understood: *Unterzeebooten*. He stared at Halfhyde, his face deeply troubled now. He said, 'It makes no kind of sense ... submarines, on the Amazon!'

'It could be done. It's common knowledge that the Germans have been building small undersea craft, little more than 260 tons displacement, modelled on advanced French designs and able to sustain long passages. It would be a comparatively easy matter for such craft to leave and re-enter the Amazon on the surface—they would draw very little water. In the event of war, they could make out across the trade routes with their torpedoes, sink our merchant ships and, indeed, our warships, and then return to base—with virtually no risk of being pursued by any large vessels, not at any rate inshore of the Canal Perigoso.'

Wainscott nodded. He was wide awake now. 'Not impossible, I suppose—all that. I've heard about those French designs ... armament of three torpedo tubes apiece, with a capacity to carry many torpedoes for reloading—'

'That's right. I'm convinced the Germans are preparing for their arrival, which probably won't be till the base construction is complete, by which time it'll be a *fait accompli*.' Halfhyde paused. 'Well? What now, Commander?'

Wainscott said, 'That paybook. It's good evidence, of course. It could be a clincher. There's a difficulty, though: the way you obtained it.'

Halfhyde shrugged. 'Needs must, Commander.'

'Yes, but you're well aware of the Brazilian order. I repeat, there's a very real difficulty, Halfhyde.'

'Yes. As it happens, there's another one.'

Wainscott looked up interrogatively.

'I appear to have lost Todhunter.'

'*Lost* him? The river?'

'Perhaps. I can't be sure. A search must be made at first light, and we must watch for a body drifting past on the current.' Halfhyde explained the circumstances fully. 'There are, of course, the alligators ... I regret having allowed him to come. I take all responsibility upon myself, I need hardly say.'

'The Germans?'

'I don't believe so. There was no one about, as I said. Todhunter is a very unhandy person. I fear a slip in the mud when he shifted berth from beside the tree, against my explicit orders.'

'It's very unfortunate, Halfhyde. I can only—' Wainscott broke off as there was a commotion outside his cabin, some argument and raised voices, one of them recognizable as that of Admiral Watkiss—and on the heels of the noise Watkiss entered with Mayhew behind him.

Wainscott got to his feet. 'Good morning, Admiral—'

'Such damned impertinence!'

'I beg your pardon, sir?'

Admiral Watkiss lifted a foot and stamped it hard on the deck. 'To send that woman! Whose idea was it, may I ask? Yours, I presume, Mr Halfhyde. A harlot, to suborn me from my duty! A painted hussy.' He was breathing heavily and thrusting here and there with his telescope. 'I would have repaired aboard earlier had it not been for the blasted rain—I was forced to take shelter in a building behind the jetty until it stopped. Now I'm here for your explanation, Mr Halfhyde, and I demand it quickly. Well, man?'

Halfhyde met Commander Wainscott's eye. Behind Admiral Watkiss, Mayhew was looking harassed, as though all diplomacy was in danger of being thrown to the winds, muttering something about the orders of the Brazilian government being ignored. Halfhyde had worse news for him; for Watkiss as well. He said, 'I think, sir, explanations should be left for the moment—'

'Oh, balls and bang me arse, Mr Halfhyde, you are just as obstructive as you always were

214

when under my command—'

'A moment, sir.' Halfhyde's tone was firm and loud. 'I have evidence that in my view incriminates the Germans and it has become necessary for Mayhew to act in the name of the British government. I think the moment of decision has come for you as well, sir, and you would do well to recognize the fact. We're going to need the assistance of a friend at court in Brazil—a friend of Her Majesty's.'

CHAPTER FOURTEEN

It was Mayhew who, despite his diplomatic training, put his foot in it. His two-way gaze straddled Halfhyde and he remonstrated with urgency. 'Captain Halfhyde, you should not speak so freely in the presence of a Brazilian—'

'What—confounded—cheek!' Admiral Watkiss swung round upon the diplomat, face almost purple. 'I am *not* a blasted Brazilian, you—you—'

'I was about to add the word representative, Admiral.'

'Oh. I see. It was still blasted cheek.' Watkiss simmered for a while. No one interrupted: much depended upon his reactions in the next few mintues. 'Well, Mr Halfhyde, perhaps you would be good enough to explain, and we shall

215

take no damn notice of this fellow Mayhew. Kindly proceed.'

Halfhyde did so, rendering a full report and making no bones about the fact that he had gone deliberately against the orders from Senhor Peixoto that no one was to leave the ship. Admiral Watkiss grew angrier.

'Blast you, Mr Halfhyde, you have put my position in jeopardy!'

'I'm sorry, sir. I was acting for the Crown.'

'Don't be so damn unctuous and mealy-mouthed, Mr Halfhyde. It ill becomes you.'

'But I repeat it, sir. The whole purpose of the *Taronga Park*'s voyage was to establish the facts about the German construction work, and I consider I have established them. It now becomes necessary in the interest of British security that there should be frank discussion between the national representatives on each side. And I believe you yourself can actually sit, as it were, in the middle.'

'You don't seem to realize my position, Mr Halfhyde, blast you!'

Halfhyde said placatingly, 'I believe I do, sir, only too well. For a start I suggest we go to my quarters. There's more room and more comfort.' In Wainscott's cabin there was no room to swing a cat and the air was close and stuffy. 'After you, sir.'

'Will that woman be there? Our discussions
216

must be in private, Mr Halfhyde.'

'They will be, sir. Miss Penn will leave the cabin.'

'Thank God for that, Mr Halfhyde, thank God for that.'

ii

Like British seamen, German seamen were at times unruly and merited cell punishment. One of the first buildings to be constructed at the base had been a punishment block with small and individual cells and, in one of these, Mr Todhunter had been confined with an armed sentry placed on the door. Cell was not quite the word; the walls were of wood, but it was substantial. It was also wet, for the small window placed high up had not yet been glazed, only barred, and the rain had been beating in unmercifully. Mr Todhunter sat in a damp patch on a wooden bench, feeling desperate and lonely. But also self-congratulatory, because he had remained mute under interrogation carried out by Captain von Grützner in person, which was probably lucky since the German was a gentleman and had behaved as such. No rough stuff, no malarkey, and Mr Todhunter was grateful. It had seemed almost ungracious to refuse to answer, but Todhunter knew his duty as always and he believed Captain von Grützner had respected him for it. Of course, the Germans were in a somewhat cleft stick; their

217

country was friendly towards Great Britain, on the surface that was, and ill-treatment of British subjects would not be popular. Mr Todhunter was naturally aware that had things been different then Captain von Grüzner might well have forgotten that he was a gentleman.

But what now?

Mr Todhunter brooded on the wet bench. Bother take it, the wet had penetrated, allowing him no chance to dry out his bottom, and he might well suffer an attack of lumbago, a painful affliction, which would add to his discomfort. One worry was the reaction of Mr Millington, who would probably disown him when the Germans made enquiries from the Brazilians. Or perhaps he wouldn't: that Admiral Watkiss might put in a word if he was taken into consultation by his Brazilian superiors and learned that the Germans had their hands on a detective inspector from Scotland Yard. He might put pressure on the consul to support Todhunter's story—or again he might not. He might act wholly in the Brazilian interest, mightn't he? He might know where his onions grew best, after all...

It was such a worry, such a quandary, and Mr Todhunter was hungry too—and wanted to relieve himself badly by this time, but the cell contained no facilities. Mr Todhunter sat with firmly crossed legs, squeezing. The dark trousers were very uncomfortable; also they were sartorially out of keeping with his soaked blue serge jacket and Mr Todhunter had felt at a disadvantage in front of Captain von Grützner, who had been beautifully uniformed and very clean, even his beard appearing as though it was given a daily trim by a barber.

Todhunter got to his feet and called out, 'I say!' There was no response. He banged on the door and called out again. Still no response: possibly the sentry had no English—you had to be broad-minded and accept that—but why not answer a bang? Todhunter's need was very great; and he began to think that the sentry must have 'been withdrawn and that he was being left utterly alone in his predicament.

iii

'You made out he'd been a bloody lecher, mate didn't you?' Victoria hissed into Halfhyde's ear outside the cabin. 'I did me best for you, I reckon. It wasn't my fault—'

'I didn't say it was, Victoria. Anyway, it doesn't matter now, it's resolved itself into something trickier and it looks as though things will shortly come to a head.'

'For the old bloke?'

'For all of us—'

'Well, just so long as I don't have to bloody go through anything like that again and get bloody insulted! D'you know something, eh? For all the reaction I got, mate, he might as well have had it bloody bitten off by a crocodile!'

Halfhyde made a tut-tutting sound and went back into his cabin where a good deal of argument was in progress and Mayhew was looking beside himself with anxiety. Admiral Watkiss was in no mood to accept diplomacy and was being adamant about two things at once: one, that the Brazilians were a bunch of dagoes who had never had the decency to inform him, as Commander-in-Chief of their blasted navy, of the true purpose, as reported by Halfhyde anyway, of the base construction; two, he had carefully to consider his own position, which could be precarious if he upset the Brazilians.

'Such an untrustworthy lot, doncher know, Mr Halfhyde. Unpredictable, too. Swayed this way and that at the drop of a blasted hat, like all damn foreigners of course.'

Halfhyde coughed. 'Perhaps you could sway them, sir?'

'In which direction for God's sake? Oh, I realize what you're trying to say, of course I do, but how the devil can I sway them against their blasted base? Can you tell me that, Mr Halfhyde?'

'There may be ways, sir.'

'*What* ways?'

'Subterfuge.' Halfhyde glanced at Mayhew. 'It shouldn't be beyond any diplomat's capability to, shall we say, indicate firmly what might be considered the wishes of Her Majesty in regard to the German Navy being given facilities—if it was reported to her that the President of Brazil was conniving against the interest of her government. What do you say, Mr Mayhew?'

Mayhew looked put out. 'I say nothing whatsoever, Captain Halfhyde—'

'Just like the blasted Foreign Office!' Admiral Watkiss let his monocle drop from his eye in disgust.

'And diplomacy is in any case not the concern of a shipmaster,' Mayhew said angrily.

'In that case I shall not attempt to be diplomatic. I have a regard for my ship and my crew—and for Mr Todhunter, who may have sacrificed his life in the interest of what we have all come here to do. It's vital—I dare say we're all agreed on this—that the affair be brought to a conclusion favourable to the British government. I believe I know a way in which that can be done, gentlemen.' Halfhyde paused, looking steadily at Mayhew. 'I have been informed by Admiral Watkiss that there are certain suspicions about Mr Millington—'

'That was not intended for the ears of your blasted diplomat, Mr Halfhyde!'

'I am sorry to break a confidence, sir. But I regard it as necessary now. If Millington is in any way acting against the British interests he is here to represent and protect, and if it can be

221

shown that he is involved for gain with the Brazilian authorities, then the public washing of dirty linen could have a salutary effect.'

'In what way, Mr Halfhyde?'

Halfhyde said, 'Other countries, when the news was made known, would find an interest in the base. The United States might not welcome a German presence to their south. Other South American states might also find objections. It's very possible that Brazil's trade would suffer world-wide. There could be many repercussions—once the diplomatic machinery got under way. I think, gentlemen, the time has come for a word in the ear of our consul. Or perhaps that of Senhor Peixoto, whose name has cropped up before now aboard my ship. As you know very well, Mr Mayhew.'

There was a silence: Halfhyde knew his words had been a catalyst of a kind. Mayhew was considering the diplomatic aspect, Admiral Watkiss was concerned that no mud should cling to his own person. Wainscott, too, had an inward look as though wondering, if things should take a dangerous turn, whether his naval guard would be required to mount a defence of the *Taronga Park*. It was into this fraught silence that the sound of footsteps fell and a few moments later the gangway watchman entered together with a sweating Brazilian.

'I am really very much obliged,' Mr Todhunter said. '*Very* much obliged.' Emerging from a latrine, he felt a good deal better. Just as matters had grown really desperate, the sentry had returned along with the petty officer of the guard, a man who spoke a few words of English and to whom Todhunter had been able to explain his need. However, it appeared that the petty officer's visit had been for a more official purpose and after he had had his pee Mr Todhunter was again required by Captain von Grützner. He was marched before him like a sinning seaman and made to stand to attention throughout; and this time von Grützner, who was accompanied by a man lurking in the background and wearing civilian clothes, was both formal and formidable.

'I have been in communication with the British consul at Santarem, Herr Todhunter.'

'Ah . . .' Todhunter felt a shake in his hands and he did his best to conceal it.

'He repudiates your story, the one that you are attached to the British consulate.'

'Oh dear!'

'You come from the *Taronga Park*, is this not so?'

Todhunter swallowed. They knew it all, so what was the use? He said, 'Yes, that is right, sir.'

'Why did you tell lies, Herr Todhunter?'

'I'm very sorry, sir, very sorry indeed.' The rain had started again now and was battering on the corrugated-iron roof and sounding llike a firing squad. Mr Todhunter shook with apprehension. He had already been told, he remembered, that he was now in German sovereign territory, far indeed from the long arm of the British law.

Von Grüzner was growing impatient. 'I asked you a question, Herr Todhunter. You will answer it. *Why?*'

'I was doing my duty, sir.'

'What duty?' The rain battered more than ever and the day grew dark, then darker. Now Captain von Grützner's beard had a Machiavellian aspect, a cruel, barbaric look fitting to the age-old cloak of Attila the Hun.

'My duty ... not to reveal anything, sir.'

'Which was scarcely your only duty, Herr Todhunter. You are a policeman from London, unless that too was a lie—'

'Oh no, sir, no. I do assure you—'

'Very well, then. Now: what was your duty to be?'

'I'm sorry to say I have no real idea, sir.'

Captain von Grützner smote his desk angrily with a sunbrowned fist. 'But you are being ridiculous! How can you not know what your duty was?'

Todhunter took a deep breath and blew it out again. How could he explain? He did his best.

'Scotland Yard, sir, is a very funny place. Not that the criminal fraternity would say so, of course. But for policemen, sir, all is not—not straightforward like. Often the orders are, well, imprecise, and persons of my rank, sir, are left to make decisions for themselves. I don't know if you follow, sir . . .' Mr Todhunter floundered on, well aware that he was cutting no ice at all. Captain von Grützner was tapping with a pencil now and there was a sardonic look in his eye as though he were letting Todhunter go on and on incriminating himself, or perhaps even finding enjoyment in his victim's verbal contortions— that cruel look! Mr Todhunter had always understood that the German officer corps was sadistic and uncaring of human life—but surely they wouldn't put him to death, not really to death, with a British ship only just down the river? They would never take the risk—there would be reprisals, and they were not fools. The British Navy itself was at hand, as represented by Commander Wainscott and his armed seamen, and Captain Halfhyde who was a lieutenant of the Royal Naval Reserve as well as being master of the *Taronga Park*—and what about Mr Mayhew of the Foreign Office?

Mr Todhunter felt courage grow within himself: he was not really alone, far from it. He would make a stand and Britain would respond. He cleared his throat and pulled himself straighter, braced his shoulders beneath the blue serge and felt the wet flap of the white duck trousers around his ankles.

He said in a firm voice, the voice almost of arrest, 'I have given all the explanations required of me by law, sir. International law as I understand it. I'm very sorry but I am not permitted to say anything further, and I would be much obliged if I could now be released and returned to where I should be, which is the *Taronga Park* in Santarem.'

Captain von Grützner seemed about to speak—from the look on his face Todhunter made the assessment that he was about to refuse the request—when he was addressed by the lurking civilian person and he turned with an air of impatience.

'Ja, Herr Naumann?'

A longish conversation in German followed. There was a show of temper from von Grützner; Mr Todhunter reflected on the similarity between naval officers of all nationalities. They all disliked civilians, Captain von Grützner as much as Admiral Watkiss now of the Brazilian Navy. Mr Todhunter listened intently even though he knew he couldn't follow: it was in the nature of detective inspectors to listen simply because you never could tell what you might pick up. And indeed, Todhunter *did* pick something up, for what it might be worth: there was a lot of discussion involving two names—Millington and Peixoto.

They came across quite clearly. Well, no doubt they were germane to his, Todhunter's, personal presence in Santarem, but there just might be something else. Peixoto was the name of the Brazilian Minister of Army and Marine, to be sure, but it was also—or from the available evidence might be—the name of the disintegrated corpse in the *Taronga Park*'s cable locker. And Todhunter was aware of other matters also: such for instance as the rumour, unsubstantiated but it could be absolutely true, that Mr Millington had been carrying on with a niece of the Minister of Army and Marine. And doubts had been cast upon the loyalty of Mr Millington.

It could be nasty. It could be very nasty indeed, but for the British rather than the Germans. An idea had come into Mr Todhunter's head; he would need to be extremely cautious in pursuing it in case he put his foot in it, but he believed it might be worth the candle. If he could contrive somehow to get at some information that, if ever he got his freedom back, might be useful to his own side, his torment would not have been in vain.

Excitement rose in him and he broke into the conversation.

'Beg pardon, sir.'

Captain von Grützner swung round. 'What is it, Herr Todhunter?'

'The name, sir. The name Peixoto.'

227

'What about it, Herr Todhunter?'

'I heard mention, sir, between you and the civilian gentleman.'

'Yes?'

'Also of Mr Millington.'

'Yes. So, Herr Todhunter?'

Todhunter opened his mouth, then closed it again. He had run out of steam, his idea had evaporated and he hadn't now, the least notion of what he had intended saying, of how he had ever had any hope that he might prise anything out of the Germans. Whatever had come over him? He breathed hard, felt a funny flutter in the region of his heart. He had aroused interest and now they wouldn't rest. What a fool he had been!

CHAPTER FIFTEEN

The Brazilian who had come aboard the *Taronga Park* had been running and was much out of breath, his chest and stomach heaving and his moustache dripping sweat.

He addressed himself to Admiral Watkiss, speaking in Portuguese.

'Oh, balls and bang me arse, these blasted dagoes! For God's sake, man, speak in *English*, can't you!'

Mayhew stepped forward. 'It's all right,

Admiral. Leave it to me!'

'Can you speak their damn lingo?'

'Yes—'

'Never said so before.' Watkiss glared around, truculently. 'Very well, then, find out what it's all about and report to me.'

The Brazilian turned to the Foreign Office man and spoke rapidly, crossing himself at intervals and rolling his eyes upwards. He appeared to be in a state of terror. It took Mayhew some while to get his story in any degree of coherence, and when he had done so he, too, appeared to be in a state of nerves and general anxiety.

'Well, what is it?' Watkiss demanded.

'A most serious matter, Admiral. Your people—'

'What people?'

'The Brazilians—'

'Bah!'

'A number of them have attacked the consulate—'

'*What?*'

'And the consul has been killed, murdered! By these men, who then made good their escape.'

Watkiss' mouth dropped open. He screwed his monocle into his eye. 'What—what—'

'This man,' Mayhew said, indicating the messenger, 'was unseen by the marauders. He is an employee at the consulate, a gardener, I gather.' Mayhew pursed his lips and looked accusingly at Watkiss. 'Admiral, I must ask for some explanation of this—this terrible act against the representative of Great Britain—'

'Don't blasted well ask *me* for an explanation!'

'Your country—'

'Don't be impertinent, if you please, Mr Mayhew—'

'Admiral, this is no time for nonsensical utterances—they simply do not help. A most serious situation has arisen—'

'I think I warned you—or did I tell Mr Halfhyde or someone?—that Millington might be under some sort of threat because of—' Watkiss broke off. Some things were perhaps better left unsaid. 'I think you can judge from that where *my* loyalties lie, you and your blasted Foreign Office, a bunch of—'

'Yes, yes—'

'*Bums*,' Admiral Watkiss said in a loud voice, determined to make his point, 'and that's fact, I said it.'

'Have it your own way, Admiral,' Mayhew said angrily. He went on quickly before there was another interruption. 'There's something else. This man made another report. That policeman, it seems he's in German hands. Captain von Grützner has been in touch by the field telegraph, which is laid on poles across the river to some kind of local post office, I

230

understand—'

'If you'll kindly stop trying to teach your grandmother—I *am* aware of certain facts pertaining to Brazil. Now then.' Admiral Watkiss flourished his telescope. 'Commander Wainscott, I understand you have a party of seamen embarked, with rifles?'

'Yes, sir.'

'For just such an occasion as this, I fancy!'

'A little late in the day, sir.'

'Better late than never, Commander. At the very least the consulate must be protected. It could be sacked, burned to the ground for all we know. Also there's poor Millington—the body. That, too, must be protected against the blasted dagoes. Kindly waste no time, Commander.'

'One moment,' Mayhew said, stepping forward. He seemed highly agitated. 'My superiors in the Foreign Office—'

'Oh, balls to the Foreign Office, my dear fellow, they—'

Mayhew interrupted loudly, his eyebrows weaving above the bony face and the squint. 'We must on no account precipitate fighting! It would be disastrous, an act of war against Brazil. To send armed sailors ashore in a foreign land would be an act of sheer provocation, Admiral.'

Watkiss sneered and thrust about with his telescope. 'Lily livers abound, it seems! Who's

231

done the provoking in the first instance, may I ask—who but the blasted dagoes?'

'I think you should remember your own position, Admiral. I think you should use the field telegraph and ask the nearest Brazilian army command for troops. That would be the proper thing to do, I assure you.' Mayhew paused; there was an inward look in Watkiss' eye now. Some progress had perhaps been made, the rigid nautical mind of Admiral Watkiss penetrated by common sense or at any rate by self-interest. Mayhew, breathing a shade easier, went on. 'There is the policeman, Todhunter, in German hands as we now know. He poses a problem, you'll agree—'

'God alone knows why he was ever sent,' Watkiss said huffily, 'unless it was simply to become a problem—' He broke off suddenly and stood ears a-cockbill. 'Shouting! Do you hear it? Mob violence! The consulate under further attack!' He swung round on Wainscott. 'As Commander-in-Chief of the Brazilian Navy I am commandeering the handiest force to protect British property! You shall mount a show of strength, my dear Wainscott, and the devil take that wretched man Mayhew!'

ii

Halfhyde was not going to be left out. He sent for Briggs while Petty Officer Parker mustered his armed party. 'Mr Briggs, you'll take over

232

the ship. I'm assuming my RNR commission and rank.'

'Aye, aye, sir.'

'If there's any trouble, if the ship's attacked, you'll haul off into the stream—warn Mr Bannion that he's to bring his engine to immediate notice as fast as possible.' Halfhyde, assisted by Barsett, was already pulling on his white uniform with the RNR insignia on the shoulder-straps. When the first mate had left the cabin to pass the orders to the bosun and the chief engineer Victoria grew tearful.

'Take care, mate, eh?'

'I will.'

'It's not your bloody fight.'

'I intend to keep an eye on Watkiss.'

'Bull in a china shop!'

'That's why I mean to keep an eye on him, Victoria.'

'Well, I think it's bloody daft. Think the old bloke'll go anywhere near danger, do you?'

He nodded. 'I do indeed. He's no coward. I have to try to stop his excesses—such as killing a Brazilian in the heat of the moment and then finding himself stripped of his rank and facing a firing squad!'

'Mean he needs a bloody nanny?'

'Yes—but take care not to say that in his hearing.'

'Well, mate, do take care. I—I reckon I'd be bloody lost if anything happened to you.'

233

He took her in his arms briefly and kissed her. 'I'll be all right, don't worry. For my money, the mob will fade away as soon as they see British seamen advancing. It'll be over in no time.'

'What about the Germans, eh, and that poor little copper?'

'First things first,' Halfhyde answered. 'He's unlikely to come to any immediate harm now he's well away from the river.' He left the cabin and went down fast to the well-deck and the gangway to the shore. The naval guard, in full white uniforms with belts and gaiters, and with rifles with bayonets fixed, were already fallen in on the jetty, a formidable bunch of seasoned men, with Petty Officer Parker standing ready in front of the files. Commander Wainscott, also in uniform, was being harangued by Admiral Watkiss who once again was thrusting this way and that with his telescope, as though making passes with a sword. Mr Mayhew stood watching from the deck, frustratedly, his wise counsels ignored by stupid fighting men who, he believed, would live to regret their impulsive actions. By this time the shouting had increased and the area contiguous to the jetty was deserted. From time to time a shot was heard, followed by wild cheering.

Watkiss stopped in mid-sentence as he saw Halfhyde.

'Make haste, Mr Halfhyde, make haste I say!

234

The buggers are already out of hand!'

'They'll soon be in our grip, sir. And I suggest you keep close by my side. I'd not like to see you take a bullet.'

'Oh, they won't shoot at me, I'm—er ...' Watkiss seemed uncertain whether to say he was British or Brazilian; he compromised by adding, 'respected, doncher know.'

'There is still a risk, sir.'

'Yes, perhaps, but best foot foremost, Mr Halfhyde.' Admiral Watkiss reached up to put a heavy hand on Halfhyde's shoulder. 'You're a stout fellow and a good friend. I have said so before.'

'Then I failed to hear you,' Halfhyde murmured as he turned away to fall in beside Wainscott as Petty Officer Parker gave the guard the order to right-turn into their line of advance. With Watkiss twinkling along on his short legs, the party moved off along the jetty, the gunner's mate calling the step loudly. The wooden jetty trembled to the co-ordinated rhythm of the marching boots. Admiral Watkiss moved to come up alongside Wainscott as they left the jetty and marched along the dusty track behind.

'Commander, I think the men should sing.'

'Sing, sir?'

Watkiss nodded. 'Something stirring. Put the fear of God into the dagoes. Same effect as the bagpipes, you see.'

235

'Aye, aye, sir.'

Wainscott turned and passed the order to the gunner's mate. The men began singing with a will, led by Parker's loud tones.

We don't want to fight but, by Jingo, if we do
We've got the ships, we've got the men,
we've got the money too...

'Splendid!' Admiral Watkiss said with tears in his eyes. 'Splendid.'

iii

At the German base the field telegraph had brought its urgent message across the river and this had been reported to Captain von Grützner who was plainly displeased. He spoke in English to Mr Todhunter.

'Your ship has landed armed seamen.'

'Oh dear, sir!' Todhunter's voice was high. Now the fat was really in the fire, an armed conflict! Still, they couldn't blame him for that. On the other hand, he might well get caught in the cross-fire, not literally he hoped, but metaphorically. What would Captain von Grützner do now?

Von Grützner went on, 'The Brazilians ask for the assistance of my men to combat the British.' He seemed to be speaking half to himself, but since he was soliloquizing in

English Mr Todhunter believed he was seeking some sort of guidance in the matter from an Englishman, an authoritative officer of the law.

He said, 'Yes, I see, sir. May I ask, sir, what you propose to do?'

There was a harsh laugh. 'One thing I do not propose to do is to start a war, Herr Todhunter!'

'Quite, sir, yes indeed.' It was encouraging, Todhunter thought. 'I think that's wise, sir. His Excellency your Emperor, sir—'

'Yes, yes.'

'And His Excellency's exalted royal grandmother.' Todhunter paused. 'Family love, sir.'

Von Grützner said something that sounded like 'Pish'. Mr Todhunter realized the German was suffering a degree of uncertainty; but believed that he would in the circumstances of the base find it untactful not to answer the Brazilian plea for assistance. Von Grützner would, in fact, be in something of a cleft stick, and the best place for him, Mr Todhunter thought with unusual venom.

Von Grützner, leaving Mr Todhunter under the ready rifle of one of his seamen, stalked away with the civilian gentleman who had uttered nothing further since his initial harangue. A few minutes later there were shouts followed by running feet and then a clank of what sounded like weapons. There

237

were more shouts and then Mr Todhunter found himself hustled about like a criminal being pushed into a Black Maria, out of the office building and into the terrible mud left behind by the rain. He protested but no one took any notice and then he found himself all mixed up with armed Germans wearing caps with black ribbons streaming down their backs and leaping to rigid attention every time an officer appeared. These men were, it seemed, being formed up into some sort of order and the officer who had first interviewed Mr Todhunter the night before was strutting about like a gilded popinjay, full of self-importance and disdainful looks, and wearing a revolver in a holster at his belt.

When the order to move off was given, Mr Todhunter found himself being marched away with the seamen, willy-nilly as to war. Down to the river and into a boat, a big one, much bigger than the lifeboat of the *Taronga Park*, with a great bell-mouthed brass funnel sticking up and emitting filthy black smoke. The journey was a painful one; the smoke blew straight down onto Mr Todhunter and made him cough, and somewhat black in the face as well. He was wedged tightly against a bulwark by the body of a very fat seaman who stank of sausage; low-growing, scrubby trees scratched past him and he cringed away in case a tree-snake should be lurking ready to pounce,

238

like a footpad from a dark alley in Soho only very much worse, of course, and very frightening indeed. A bite would mean searing pain and a swelling and his flesh going all discoloured as the serpent's poison spread along the bloodstream and almost certainly no medical gentleman for hundreds of miles of swamp and prairie. Every time the fat seaman shifted his bulky stomach, Mr Todhunter was given an extra crush and began to fear for his liver and kidneys, such valuable parts.

But all things come to an end and it was with much relief that Todhunter was borne round a bend in the river and saw Santarem ahead and the *Taronga Park* lying peacefully alongside the wooden jetty, presumably to disembark the armed men. Then from the *Taronga Park*'s bridge, he heard a shout.

'Wotcher, mate!'

Captain Halfhyde's woman—and he had been seen and recognized! He saw her waving at him. She looked worried. He raised an arm with difficulty from behind the fat seaman's bottom and waved back, but before he could call out he found himself seized from behind. A roughened hand was clamped hard upon his mouth with such force that he toppled over backwards from his seat upon a thwart and lay with legs thrashing the air and his face close to booted feet.

He heard the woman again, loudly: 'Why,

239

you rotten lot of buggers!' Mr Todhunter, upside-down, blenched; it was provocative but fortunately no one seemed to be taking any notice. The boat came alongside, the bowman and the sternsheetsman leapt onto the jetty and secured lines to the bollards, and under the shouted orders of the officer, his hand upon the butt of his holstered revolver, the seamen and Mr Todhunter began to climb out of the boat. By this time the decks of the *Taronga Park* were crowded: all hands had turned out to watch. The First Mate was on the bridge with the woman, Todhunter saw, and smoke was issuing from the tall, thin funnel abaft the bridge. Mr Todhunter, seeing the signs of apparent departure from the port, felt faint; he was going to be abandoned.

Could he reach the gangway without being apprehended or shot at? It was not all that far, but he would need to run very fast, and he was not in the peak of condition, though he had been something of a runner in his time, years ago now—being a good sportsman he had once taken part in an annual event held at the Metropolitan Police orphanage and had won the egg-and-spoon race, to the acclaim of the orphans and his own comrades of the Force, something he had never forgotten, all that rather surprised cheering ... the memory was heartening now, very heartening, and he might bring off his dash for freedom.

240

He looked around as he dragged himself up to the jetty and stood upright. It must be a split-second decision, made at precisely the right moment, and then he mustn't hesitate, just run like the wind with no backward look.

All the seamen appeared to be busy, falling in. He believed this was the moment. He took it. He ran fast for the gangway, his stomach turning to water, dreading gunfire. He was shouting out something but he didn't know what and one of the ship's crew was coming down the gangway, ready to assist him aboard. He was going to succeed. The Germans wouldn't dare...

He was within six feet of the gangway's foot when he felt himself seized by two Germans with vice-like grips, lifted into the air, turned round the other way, and taken back to the waiting files with legs kicking uselessly. British seamen stared down from the *Taronga Park* but none of them came to his assistance. There had been a rattle of rifle magazines and bolts and the barrels were pointed at the ship. Mr Todhunter prayed that the woman wouldn't utter again. This time, she might be heard.

iv

Wainscott had halted his naval guard outside the British consulate. So far Admiral Watkiss had been proved correct in his prognostications: there had been a mob, and a large one, but they

241

had moved aside to let the marching men through, persuaded partly by the coarse shouts of the gunner's mate who had no inhibitions about the use of naval language, addressing the Brazilians as greasy buggers, sods in sombreros, and the sons of whores, until Admiral Watkiss had detached Halfhyde to the rear to order Parker to hold his tongue.

'I am after all their naval Commander-in-Chief, Mr Halfhyde, and Parker's sentiments are somewhat detrimental to my own standing. Added to which, my own presence is enough to guarantee us passage through.'

'Let us hope so, sir.' In point of fact the odd stone had been cast, and one had cannoned off a rifle and caused its bearer to lurch, but that had been all. The mood, however, was plainly nasty; Halfhyde formed the opinion that the local populace knew well enough what had brought the British Navy to Santarem and they didn't want the Germans to leave; the German presence no doubt brought some temporary employment of native labour and would be a continuing source of income for the local traders who supplied foodstuffs, trinkets to be taken back to mothers and wives in Germany, and very probably brothel facilities as well.

'Brothels,' Admiral Watkiss suddenly announced.

'Two minds with but a single thought, sir,' replied Halfhyde.

242

'What?'

'No port is ever without them, sir.'

'Oh, I know that, thank you, Mr Halfhyde,' Admiral Watkiss said distantly, 'but seldom as blatant as *that* one.' He pointed to a sleazy building coming up on the left of the marching column. Blatant it was: there was a life-size depiction of a naked and well-endowed woman hoisted like a battle ensign over the roof and from no less than six windows women waved with bared breasts a-dangle over the sills. Even as Halfhyde watched, two of the women vanished, probably in response to custom from some of the mob that had lost interest in less important proceedings.

'A pity the premises aren't very much larger,' Halfhyde said with a grin.

'What? Oh, I see. Yes. Of course, these dagoes are at it all the time, virtually non-stop I fear, such misplaced energy! I find it rather disgusting.' Admiral Watkiss looked backwards, lingeringly, as the four remaining pairs of breasts drew astern. 'No moral fibre, doncher know, which is one of the problems of life out here. And something we're going to face this day, Mr Halfhyde!'

'Yes, sir?'

'Yes, Mr Halfhyde. Millington's whispered disloyalty ... he was no doubt suborned by unprincipled people, damn dagoes with no sense of decency—as I said, no moral

243

fibre—and then, of course, there's the question of Millington's peccadillo—the affair with the Peixoto woman.'

'Are we sure of that, sir?'

'Yes! *I* am, anyway. Blasted fornicator! So stupid, a man in his position, a position of trust.'

'It could be turned to our advantage, I fancy.'

'I fail to see how, Mr Halfhyde. Dirt is dirt, nothing else. It clings where it sticks, if you follow.' Admiral Watkiss scratched at his chin. 'Makes a man wide open to blackmail among other things. These dagoes don't like their women interfered with, doncher know, they're very possessive.'

'Even a niece?'

'What?'

'The woman involved, sir, is said to be a niece of Senhor Peixoto—'

'Yes, quite. Yes, even a niece—honour is at stake, you see. And there may have been a—a suitor who would feel aggrieved I presume. Indeed, it seems to me obvious that poor Millington's murder was due to his carrying on, don't you agree, Mr Halfhyde?'

'It seems likely, sir, but we should not pre-judge.'

'Oh, quite. But I tell you one thing, Mr Halfhyde, and it's this: I shall use my position as Commander-in-Chief of the navy to ensure that the consulate's gone through with a toothcomb. Documents and so on. Something may emerge.'

Halfhyde lifted an eyebrow and looked sideways at Watkiss, whose face was puce beneath the cocked hat. 'Diplomatic immunity, sir? Immunity from search by the host power?'

'Oh, what balls, Mr Halfhyde. Power! Piddling lot of dagoes!'

'But—'

'There are no buts, my dear fellow, and that's fact, I said it.'

They marched on; soon, after passing by an open sewer and a slaughterhouse, they were able to see the consulate, with more mob outside the gates. Approaching closer, Commander Wainscott gave the order to halt and turn into line. As the guard was stood easy before the gates, Wainscott, avoiding both the gates and the mob, went forward alone, skirting the concentration of shouting, gesticulating Brazilians to head for the perimeter fence. When after a searching look around the compound he turned and came back Halfhyde went forward to meet him.

'Well, Commander?'

Wainscott said, 'Three bodies, lying in the sun. I believe one of them is Millington but I can't be sure.'

'And the others?'

Wainscott shrugged. 'Consulate staff, locals, though frankly I'd have expected them to bugger off the moment there was trouble. It looks to me as though the mob broke through but pulled back again.'

'No other British?'

'No. Santarem's a backwater—or has been, until now. Well, I'd better report to the Admiral—it's his country!' As Wainscott turned away, Watkiss was already approaching, his monocle screwed into place and his telescope held like a club. Dust rose around his feet.

Wainscott made his report. Watkiss nodded importantly and said, 'Very well, we shall enter. I have the right,' he added with a glare at Halfhyde. 'Not the guard. You and I, Wainscott, and Mr Halfhyde.'

'What shall we do, sir?'

'Our duty, Commander. We shall investigate and search. And we shall lose no time. I'd not be surprised if that bugger Peixoto turns up at any blasted moment and I mean to get in ahead of him.'

Admiral Watkiss moved towards the mob standing between him and the gateway. There was a stir and a murmur as his intentions became obvious; unlike the first Englishman, the little fat one was making straight for the gate.

'Make way there!' Admiral Watkiss shouted, waving his telescope.

There was laughter, rude and derisive, and

not a man or woman moved. A small boy put his thumb to the tip of his nose and waggled his fingers, laughing shrilly.

'Damn dagoes!' Watkiss was losing his temper; if it went altogether, anything might happen. Halfhyde moved up to stand alongside Watkiss, who looked aside irritably. 'I can manage on my own, thank you, Mr Halfhyde.' He raised his voice again, addressing the mob, whom he found smelled very strongly of sweat and dirt. The sun was high now and Watkiss felt stifled, which worsened his temper, as did the sight of a mangy dog with bared, yellow teeth that had wandered onto the scene in the way of dogs at solemn occasions. 'You will give me access to the gate, blast you! I—'

'I doubt if they speak English, sir,' Halfhyde murmured in his ear.

Watkiss stamped his foot. 'Oh, balls and bang me arse, Mr Halfhyde, I know they don't *understand* it, but they damn well get the drift! And they know quite well who I am.' To underline precisely who he was, he told them. 'I am the Commander-in-Chief of the Brazilian Navy, the personal representative presently in Santarem of you—my—our—the President, President Dr Manuel Ferraz de Campos Salles. In his name I command you to blasted well bugger off from the gateway! Damn! Oh, *damnation!*' Watkiss bent towards the ground; Halfhyde watched with interest. The Admiral's

247

monocle had shot from his eye and its toggle had parted. 'It's broken, Mr Halfhyde! Broken, blast it!'

'A tragedy, sir.'

'A strong word, but it's certainly a blasted nuisance. Look at that bunch!'

'Yes, sir.' No one had moved despite the clarity of utterance of the President's name. 'A show of strength, sir?'

'The guard, Mr Halfhyde?'

'I think so, sir.'

'A token, then. No firing.'

'Aye, aye, sir.' Smartly Halfhyde turned about and approached Wainscott, who passed the order to the gunner's mate. With a rattle from the fixed bayonets, the rifles came up to the firing position and were aimed point-blank into the mob. Immediately this had the desired effect: the mob parted to right and left, not even hurling abuse, but moving away rapidly and in a scared silence.

Watkiss was preening now. 'Nothing like the British tar, Mr Halfhyde! Such splendid fellows, splendid to a man! I shall now enter, and you will follow.'

Admiral Watkiss advanced towards the gate followed by Wainscott and Halfhyde. Taking the next move upon himself, Petty Officer Parker ordered the rifles to the slope, turned the guard into line, and marched them round until they were across the gateway itself, when

248

he halted them and once again turned them into line with their backs to the gate and the rifles pointing outwards to cover the crowd which had withdrawn to a safer distance but were still very much in the vicinity and needed watching. Parker stood himself easy and picked at his teeth with a matchstick drawn from a pocket and thought about the breasts drooping from the brothel's sills. Lovely. A pity there hadn't been a longer view. Petty Officer Parker was something of a brothel connoisseur, a good brothel hand whose experience extended from Queen Street, Pompey, to Hong Kong and Weihaiwei. The inhabitants of brothels came in all shapes and sizes and all colours, but there was something about Brazilian women that already told Parker they might appeal strongly, a case of novelty since he had never before been in a South American port. Maybe there would be a chance later, when that Admiral Watkiss in his comic-opera rig had sorted things out, though currently it was hard to know whose side he was on anyway.

While Parker pursued hopeful thoughts of shore-side dalliance, Admiral Watkiss was making for the consulate entrance past the three bodies lying in the dust. The sun was getting to work: and they could have been there for some time for all Watkiss knew. Dagoes never hurried when work was in prospect.

'Poor Millington, he's high already, Mr

Halfhyde.'

'Burial parties, sir—'

'Well, the ground should be soft enough after all that rain, but first things first, Mr Halfhyde.' Admiral Watkiss bounced on and led the way into the consulate building, a not very imposing one since Santarem was a not very important outpost of Empire, a word that Watkiss liked and was regretful that it didn't exactly apply in Brazil. The lobby was dusty and had a disagreeable smell of neglect, and the portrait of Her Majesty Queen Victoria hung askew from a picture rail.

Watkiss clicked his tongue. 'Mr Halfhyde, Her Majesty.'

'What about her, sir?'

'Damn well straighten her, Mr Halfhyde. Her position is undignified.'

Halfhyde did so, or tried to. When he lifted and shifted the portrait sideways, Queen Victoria broke away and crashed to the floor. Admiral Watkiss danced angrily in front of the wreck.

'You always were a clumsy oaf, Mr Halfhyde, and now look what you've done! I only hope to God it isn't a blasted omen!'

'I would doubt it, sir.' Halfhyde picked up the Queen and propped her against the wall: the picture rail was out of reach. 'There. Now all's well.'

The incident had upset Watkiss; there had been *lèse-majesté* and he didn't like it. Omens were still upon his mind as he progressed through the consulate and its deserted desolation. It was as though the whole Empire had crashed with Queen Victoria, and with the wretched Germans in the vicinity the whole thing boded ill. The Germans were always out to make trouble and Watkiss himself, some while ago when the question of their ostensibly innocuous presence in Brazil had first been raised in Rio de Janeiro, had gone as far as he dared in trying to keep them out of the country. His course had been—still was—a difficult one to steer if he was to avoid the rocks of dismissal from the Brazilian Navy or even summary conviction of disloyalty to the President which could lead to imprisonment or worse. It was very galling for a British subject and Admiral Watkiss always kept Lord Cochrane in mind as a consolation and example. It must have been galling to Lord Cochrane too to have been subservient to a bunch of dagoes and worse. Lord Cochrane had eventually turned Greek and fought the Turks, another filthy bunch—a very varied career and, to Admiral Watkiss, an inspiring one though he himself would certainly never have joined the Greeks in whose presence, it was said, a man needed to stand with his back well pressed against a bulkhead...

'Well now, Mr Halfhyde, the study, and poor Millington's papers.'

'Is this ethical, sir?'

'Oh, balls to whether it's ethical or not.' Admiral Watkiss bounced into the consul's study, made for a large desk set across a corner of the room and began ferreting about in the drawers. After some while he appeared to have drawn a blank.

'Fellow's been clever, Mr Halfhyde. There's nothing of any interest, nothing at all.' Watkiss paused and stared at Halfhyde, who was moving about the room looking high and low. 'What the devil are you doing, may I ask?'

'Looking for a safe, sir. There could be one concealed behind—'

'Found one?'

'No, sir.'

'Oh. Well, stop wasting time. If there is one it'll be locked, obviously.'

'And if there is one, that'll be where Millington kept his secrets, if any.'

'Yes, yes, but there doesn't seem to be one!' Watkiss gave an angry hissing sound. 'We'll try his bedroom, Mr Halfhyde. Upstairs with you, fast!'

With Wainscott, they climbed the stairs, Watkiss puffing and panting and growing ever redder in the face: the stairs were of a steeper angle than would be found in a grander consulate. The effort, however, proved worthwhile: the bedroom, or rather the dressing-room leading off it, contained a small safe found by Watkiss himself, hidden away in the recesses of a large wardrobe. Watkiss gave a triumphant shout from inside.

'Mr Halfhyde, I have it! The safe.' There was an exclamation and an expletive. 'Blasted ants, and they bite! What are they doing here, might I ask!'

'I've no idea, sir. Is the safe locked?'

'Of course it is. And blasted well bolted to the wall behind, through the woodwork. If only we had some explosive!' Admiral Watkiss emerged backwards, shedding ants.

'Let me have a look, sir.' Halfhyde brushed past and crawled into the wardrobe. It had a musty smell and the ants, big red ones, seemed legion. They appeared to have a nest in the wall behind the safe. Halfhyde laid hold of the metal and jerked at it; it gave a little, as though the wall was crumbling, but it remained otherwise fast. He crawled out.

'Loose, sir, but not loose enough. I suggest Millington may have had the keys on him—'

'A good idea, Mr Halfhyde, and we shall search the body. Down you go, and hurry.'

Halfhyde went down the stairs, across the lobby and out to the compound. Flies had settled on Millington and were disturbed by Halfhyde's approach. Bending, he extracted a bunch of keys from a trouser pocket and rejoined Admiral Watkiss with them. The fourth key seemed to fit, but not quite; Halfhyde gave it a hard turn and it jammed. It would move neither to right nor left nor could it be extracted. Halfhyde admitted defeat.

'Oh, for someone who wasn't so blasted cack-handed!'

'I'm sorry, sir. We must go back to loosening it—dig it out—a bayonet might do the trick. With your permission—'

'Oh, anything you blasted well like!' Admiral Watkiss snapped. Halfhyde went across to the window and stepped out onto a small balcony. Lifting his voice in a shout, he called for Petty Officer Parker to detach a strong seaman with rifle and bayonet and orders to report immediately to the consul's dressing-room. Admiral Watkiss was not satisfied.

'Suppose we move it out, Mr Halfhyde. How do we get into the blasted thing?'

Halfhyde shrugged. 'Once it's aboard my ship, my carpenter will deal with it easily enough, I fancy.'

'You mean we carry it all the way through the streets?'

'It can be done, sir. We have enough hands.'

'So long as it can be done before that dago bugger gets here, Mr Halfhyde.'

Within a couple of minutes, a stalwart seaman had reported and had been set to work. Heavy grunts issued from the wardrobe and there were sounds of scraping and crumbling that went on for some while. Watkiss grew more and more impatient.

'Hurry, man, hurry!'

'Doin' me best, sir. Tryin' not to bust me bayonet, sir.'

'Bugger your bayonet.'

'Aye, sir.' There was a pause, then a harsher sound than before. 'Reckon she's comin', sir.'

'Thank God. A long pull and a strong pull! Give him a hand, Mr Halfhyde, don't stand there like a whore at a wedding.'

Five minutes later success was achieved. The safe came away from the wall and was lifted out by Halfhyde and the seaman and set with a thud on the floor. 'No time to lose now,' Admiral Watkiss said. 'We march upon the *Taronga Park* and pray God we get there in time!'

CHAPTER SIXTEEN

Halfhyde was uncertain as to precisely what Admiral Watkiss expected to find in the consul's safe: when he made the enquiry as the heavy object was conveyed along the dusty street, Admiral Watkiss seemed not to know either.

'Time will tell, Mr Halfhyde, but I suspect there will be evidence.'

255

'Of what, sir?'

Watkiss looked sideways, eyebrows raised in astonishment. 'How am I blasted well expected to know until the thing has been opened? And what's that ahead, may I ask?' He felt for the missing monocle. 'Marching men, I fancy!'

'Marching men indeed, sir. Germans.'

'Blasted Huns! Are you sure, Mr Halfhyde?'

'Yes. And do you see who's in front of their line of advance?'

'No, I don't, and I don't blasted well ... Good God!' Watkiss had focused without the monocle's assistance. 'It's that man Todhunter, the policeman!' The telescope was thrashed about wildly. 'What's he been up to, I wonder? Traitorous activities I'll be bound! God, I'll have all their balls for breakfast, damned if I don't!'

'I advise caution, sir. I advise it very strongly.'

'Caution be damned! Why? Why should I be blasted cautious, I'd like to—'

'You should remember you're no longer—'

'Are you proposing to insult me again, Mr Halfhyde?'

'By no means, sir. But you no longer speak for England.'

'What balls, of course I do.'

'Then *sotto voce*, sir.'

'Oh, hold your tongue, Mr Halfhyde.' Admiral Watkiss bounced along, his short legs

256

moving rapidly as he put on speed, anxious, Halfhyde saw, to engage the enemy. Fervently, Halfhyde hoped the engagement would be confined to a duologue: the Germans had landed a force double the strength of the British contingent, and Admiral Watkiss plus the stifling heat and the humidity was bound to exacerbate tempers. Besides which, the Germans were not peaceable people at the best of times.

Admiral Watkiss, having by now placed himself well ahead of the column of seamen and slap in the German line of advance, had halted and was shouting.

'You will kindly bring your advance to a halt! Who's in charge, may I ask?' There were two officers present and Watkiss had never studied foreign uniforms, considering them to be beneath his notice. 'What are you doing there, Todhunter?'

The Germans had halted by command of their own officer, who now stood face to face with Admiral Watkiss, to whose side Halfhyde had gone supportively. Mr Todhunter answered the Admiral's question: 'I am captive, sir, not here of my own free will at all, though I really must say I'm delighted to—'

'Yes, yes, that'll be all, Todhunter. Now.' Admiral Watkiss prodded the German officer, the older of the two, with his telescope. 'You are who?'

257

'Lieutnant Dohlus—'

'A mere lieutenant,' Watkiss said disagreeably. 'Where is Captain von Grützner? Oh, don't bother to answer, it's obvious he's skulking in his blasted encampment, no guts ... I expect to be met by the senior officer of the station, not by one of his lickspittles, and if your Captain didn't know I'd be here then all I can say is, he damn well *ought* to have known, since it's the British consul who's been murdered!' Watkiss paused, chest heaving. 'Come here, Todhunter. Rejoin your own countrymen at once!'

Todhunter licked at his lips and looked nervously at the German officer, who appeared still to be trying to sort out Watkiss' tirade. Todhunter remained where he was.

'You heard my order, Todhunter.'

'Oh yes, sir, I did.'

'Then kindly obey it!'

'Well, sir, I fear the—'

'You're a lily-livered fellow, Todhunter.'

'Not lily-livered, sir, and I do beg your pardon. Frightened yes, but not—'

'Oh, hold your tongue, Todhunter, I don't bandy words with policemen.' Watkiss addressed the German again. 'Release this man at once and order him to fall in in rear of me. That is, if you don't wish to provoke an international incident, which I assure you I've more than half a mind to create! Now then.'

The German found his tongue. 'My Captain sends his sorrows, Admiral—'

'Apologies.'

'Ah, yes, apologies. I—'

'So I should blasted well think! Well, what about the policeman? The kidnap and retention of a British policeman is a most serious matter and one that—'

'He is free to leave us.'

'One that you may be sure I shall represent at the very highest level ... What did you say?'

The German bowed from the waist and clicked his heels together. 'Herr Todhunter is quite free to go, Admiral.'

'Oh. Well, why didn't you say so more clearly? Todhunter!'

'I'm very much obliged, sir, very much obliged indeed.' Mr Todhunter moved fast, mopping at his streaming face and lifting his bowler hat at Watkiss as he scuttled past to the rear. Watkiss stared the German officer up and down.

'Now, Mr What's-your-name, I speak to you as a Br—as the Brazilian Naval Commander-in-Chief who happens to owe loyalty also to Her Britannic Majesty Queen Victoria. I order that you return to your base and inform your Captain that his presence is required aboard the *Taronga Park*, is that quite clear?' This time Watkiss had remembered to speak very slowly, and, of course, loudly as was always best with

259

natives or anyone else who wasn't British. The German had an obstinate face and was looking annoyed, but Admiral Watkiss took no notice and merely gave a formal nod when the Hun saluted in acceptance of his order.

'I obey the commands of my host country, Admiral,' he said, and turned about to pass the orders meekly enough. Watkiss watched the armed party march away, back towards the jetty, then turned to Halfhyde.

'Well, Mr Halfhyde, no damn bloodshed. I think I handled that rather well. I've always taken the view that tact is best whenever possible. And thank God I was able to dispose of those Huns before that bugger Peixoto turned up! Where's that policeman?'

'Here I am, sir—'

Watkiss whirled round. 'I dislike being *stood behind*, Todhunter. Now, whilst we march back to the ship, you shall give me a full account of your sojourn with the Huns.'

ii

The march back to the jetty was accomplished without trouble. Once again Petty Officer Parker looked with strong desire at the brothel where the members of staff, busy with their duties, were no longer at the balconies. The Brazilian mob was quiescent, for which Parker thanked his rifles and bayonets. When shore leave was given the buggers would still be scared and he could preen as the Petty Officer of the British Naval Guard; the brothel might even admit him half price—he had a prestige value. Two for the price of one would be worth having. Parker sucked at a hollow tooth and gave praise where it was due: that Watkiss looked half a loony, or anyway a cross between a loony and a bomb, but he'd done his stuff all right with the Huns. Britannia ruled the waves, even in sodding Santarem, half-way up the Amazon, and even though Watkiss had taken the dago shilling, as it were, he was still full to the gunnels of good old British bull.

On arrival back aboard, dust-covered and sweating into their white uniforms, the guard was fallen out with orders to stand by for instant muster if required. Disregarding Mayhew, who was waiting by the gangway in a state of great agitation, Halfhyde ordered the four hands who had been detailed to carry the safe to take it on up to his cabin. He followed after sending the gangway watchman for the carpenter. He found Victoria pouring water into a teapot.

'Heard you coming back, mate. Thank God you're safe, eh?'

Halfhyde nodded. 'Any trouble aboard?'

'No.' She handed him a cup of tea, which he took gratefully. 'Except that Mayhew bloke . . . muttering about the Foreign Office. Reckon he doesn't trust that Watkiss an inch. He says

261

seamen haven't the right to bloody meddle. Blames you too.'

'Well, we'll not mind Mayhew. Admiral Watkiss has matters nicely in hand—at any rate until the Brazilian Minister of Army and Marine turns up.'

'Uh-huh. Where's the old bloke now, eh?'

'Engaged with Mayhew, I fancy, who was lurking by the gangway.'

'What about that safe, eh?'

'It may contain some answers,' Halfhyde said.

iii

Admiral Watkiss was in a fractious mood as the ship's carpenter got to work on the safe; he strutted up and down, looking continually from the cabin door towards the end of the jetty where there was still no sign of Arnaldo Peixoto, and irritating both Halfhyde and the carpenter with his constant adjurations to hurry. Mr Mayhew was sticking by the safe like a hairy leech, determined to vet all that came out of it. The work seemed to take an age and the cabin resounded to metallic bangs as a heavy hammer was wielded and some instrument like a jemmy was inserted the moment the door began to show a gap around one edge.

'Nearly there, sir,' the carpenter reported, hitting the end of the jemmy hard with his

262

hammer. 'Shouldn't come open at all, by rights. I reckon the metal's flawed, what I'd call poor workmanship.'

'Probably Brazilian,' Admiral Watkiss said.

There were more hefty bangs and much manoeuvring of the jemmy. Admiral Watkiss wiped his face with his handkerchief: his hands shook. Mayhew stood as if ready to pounce. Halfhyde, watching, wondered what the effect would be on Admiral Watkiss if the safe should contain nothing of interest—even, perhaps, nothing at all.

But such was not the case. The door came open.

Papers: Mayhew's hand shot out.

'Oh no you damn well don't,' Admiral Watkiss said, making a counter-snatch.

iv

Admiral Watkiss had interposed his thick body between Mayhew and the safe. There were vociferous protests from the Foreign Office man that the contents of the safe were British property; but Watkiss stood his ground, for current purposes as a high-ranking Brazilian officer in whose country the find had been made.

'The consulate,' Mayhew said savagely, '*any* British consulate, is inviolate British territory—'

'Oh, balls, *I'm* British, am I not?'

263

Mayhew looked close to tears of rage and frustration. 'You can't have it both ways!'

'Oh yes I can!'

It appeared an impasse but a compromise was reached at Halfhyde's suggestions: both Admiral Watkiss and Mr Mayhew should take the contents of the safe to the chart room, spread them out over the chart table and read them together.

'Very well,' Watkiss said disagreeably, 'but you shall come as well. I don't trust blasted diplomats as you know, they have clerks' minds, not that I have any need to take the slightest notice of them, naturally.'

'As a Brazilian, sir?'

'Don't be impertinent, Mr Halfhyde.'

All three climbed to the chart room and the safe's contents were sifted through in a preliminary operation. There was Millington's personal diary; some closely written sheets of paper, some in English, some in Portuguese; there was an official-looking document in an envelope with the seal of the government in Rio de Janeiro, and another envelope containing a great deal of money in high denomination Portuguese notes. These Admiral Watkiss, watched closely by Mr Mayhew, counted out.

'Half a million escudos! Now, what's that in British money, I wonder? Not that it matters. The point is that there's bribery and corruption in the air, and that's fact, I said it.'

'There is no evidence, Admiral—'

'Well, we'll damn well find it, won't we?' Watkiss said triumphantly. 'It'll be in all this bumph—we must lose no time in going through it. Send that policeman up, if you please, Mr Halfhyde, he can assist—and I'll tell you something else: I said earlier, did I not, that I had my suspicions as to that fellow's presence and now we damn well know! He was here to arrest Millington—he was to be handy when Millington had been exposed, don't you see? Arrest a traitor—'

'Extradition proceedings,' Mayhew began, 'are—'

'Oh, balls and bang me arse, don't always throw up difficulties and irrelevancies. Just like the blasted Foreign Office, everlastingly thinking of treaties, scraps of paper! I'm not going to be blasted well hamstrung by clerks and parchment! Must I repeat my order, Mr Halfhyde, to get Todhunter up here immediately?'

'I shall see to it at once, sir, and I advise you to get your facts together quickly. Senhor Peixoto is coming along the jetty.' Halfhyde turned from the port through which he had been looking. 'I'll do my best to hold him off until you're ready.' He left the chart room and, passing the word to Todhunter on the way, went down to the gangway to receive the Minister of Army and Marine, who was

265

accompanied by an ornate individual in a light blue uniform with many hanging golden tassels and wide epaulettes, giving his already stunted figure the aspect of a box with legs.

'Welcome aboard, Senhor Peixoto.'

'Thank you, Captain.' Peixoto turned to the square man. 'I introduce to you Colonel de Souza, Chief of Police for the state of Amazonas.'

'Ah yes.' Halfhyde shook an out-thrust hand. 'You have business aboard my ship, Colonel de Souza?'

The swarthy face remained blank; no English. Peixoto answered for him. 'There has been a murder. I believe you know this?'

'Yes.'

'There must be an investigation.'

'Of course.'

'It is a matter of some delicacy. Where is Admiral Watkiss, please? I am informed that he boarded your ship, Captain.'

'Yes. I'm afraid he's busy just at the moment. Er . . .'

Something like a sigh of exasperation came from the Minister of Army and Marine. 'Not again his stomach?'

'Er . . .'

'Always since taking service under my President, Admiral Watkiss has complained of our food, that it exacerbates his stomach and that he suffers much and inconveniently. It is

266

often inconvenient to others as well as himself.'

'I shall have him told you're aboard, Senhor Peixoto,' Halfhyde said, tongue in cheek, not committing himself as to Watkiss' stomach but hoping that the Admiral wouldn't take too long in getting at the gist of Millington's papers. He led the way up the ladder to his cabin, and summoned Barsett. Drinks were brought; toasts were drunk as before, which took up time; bottoms were shifted about on chairs, fingers drummed on handy surfaces. Halfhyde made desultory conversation, his mind on the doings of Admiral Watkiss and his helpers. Watkiss might well find nothing in the way of evidence; the whole charge against Millington could be in his mind alone. But the money spoke, of course. And there had evidently been a need for secrecy and concealment on Millington's part.

'Admiral Watkiss is paying a long visit,' Peixoto said.

'It does happen, with a change of climate.'

'And the food.'

'And the food indeed.'

'That the trouble, is it?' Victoria asked suddenly. She had been engaging the attentions, if not the conversation, of the Chief of Police, whose hand lay upon her arm and was moving a little up and down. 'Poor old bloke, eh! First time I went up from Sydney to Brisbane I got the shits for a bloody week.'

267

'Well, Todhunter?'

Mr Todhunter pursed his lips. 'Well, sir, speaking, if you follow me, as a detective inspector—'

'Yes, yes, yes!'

'Of the Metropolitan Police, if I might make the point, sir, it being of importance since strictly speaking I have no authority to act outside my area but since Mr Mayhew is present to—'

'Oh, for God's sake, Todhunter, we haven't got all blasted day!'

'Quite, sir, yes. No, I mean. Well then, sir, to cut matters short, I agree there appears to be a case, *prima facie* that is—'

'Oh, balls to *prima facie*, are you saying that you agree Millington's a traitor and an accessory to murder, or are you not?'

'Well, sir, it has to be taken into account that—'

'Oh, hold your tongue, Todhunter, if you can't be precise then *I* blasted well shall be. Millington is or was what I've just said he was, and I propose to act accordingly—why, the whole blasted thing's down there in pen and ink—and Portuguese currency!' Admiral Watkiss thumped a fist on the pile of paper. 'You can't disregard the evidence, and if Millington was still alive I'd press for his immediate arrest and Mayhew could have damn well got on with his blasted extradition rubbish, though if I had my way—'

'One moment, Admiral.' Mayhew's voice was loud and held a note of desperation; the eyes, looking two ways at once, were wild. 'You are likely to be an—an encumbrance to diplomacy, to any efforts I might make—'

'Then don't make any. You're only a blasted nuisance as I've said before. All this damn tomfoolery! I shall ask you a simple question, Mr Mayhew: are you or are you not on the side of Her Majesty?'

'What a thing to ask!'

'Try to answer it.'

'I shall answer it obliquely,' Mayhew said, his voice spiteful and furious. 'I shall say to you that you should watch your step, Admiral Watkiss, since if you press your revelations too far you will be in much local trouble. You will be seen to act against the Brazilian President. And whatever you like to think, you are now a Brazilian. What do you say to *that*?'

Watkiss was temporarily speechless; while he struggled to express himself Mr Todhunter, who had heard sounds from below and had taken a look through the port, spoke in a voice high with agitation.

'The German gentleman, sir—'

'What about him?'

'He has arrived, sir. Captain von Grützner, in a boat.'

'Ha! Has he indeed! Pray do not look so blasted terrified, Todhunter. You are aboard a British ship. And so am I.' Admiral Watkiss, who had now co-ordinated his line of attack to come, bared his teeth at Mayhew. 'We shall see what we shall see. Let us go down to Halfhyde's cabin and meet the dago and the Hun, damn foreigners filled with tricks as a monkey is with fleas!'

Admiral Watkiss proceeded down the ladder to the Master's deck, his long shorts flapping about his knees in a light but welcome breeze, a rather smelly one since it was coming off Santarem. He entered the cabin as Halfhyde reached the well-deck to greet von Grützner. The Minister of Army and Marine waved a hand at Watkiss but didn't get to his feet, which was annoying.

'Good morning, Senhor Peixoto. You'll excuse my not being present on your arrival.'

'You are better?'

'Better?' Watkiss was bewildered, then he ticked over. 'You refer to my wretched time at the end of the jetty no doubt. A wearisome experience I'll admit, and an improper and unfair one though perhaps to be expected of . . . I was left there all night like some blasted ordinary seaman! But yes, I have recovered, thank you.'

'He didn't mean that,' Victoria said. This was a fine opportunity to get some of her own back

270

on the old bloke and his hurtful attitude during the night watch. 'He meant you had the—'

'When I wish you to interpret I shall say so,' Admiral Watkiss broke in snappishly. The woman looked like going on further but was silenced by the arrival of Halfhyde with Captain von Grützner in tow. Watkiss swung round. 'Good morning, Captain von Grützner. You have arrived at a fruitful moment.'

There was a click of uniformed heels and a tight bow. 'How, fruitful?'

'Very fruitful. I have evidence of bribery and corruption on an immense scale.' Admiral Watkiss paused; he noted the signs of unease from the Minister of Army and Marine. Mayhew started to speak but Watkiss cut him short. 'Hold your tongue, if you please, Mr Mayhew. Bribery and corruption, I said. Also murder, and connivance at murder. It is well documented, and the documents are in my possession and will remain there until they have been deposited with the proper authorities in Great Britain. Yes, Senhor Peixoto?'

Peixoto had been showing further signs of unease; his eyes were dangerous. 'Who are you accusing, Admiral Watkiss? What does all this mean?'

'You will see shortly, Senhor, and so will von Grützner. I ask you a question, Senhor Peixoto: does the name Otto Leber convey anything to you?'

'Otto Leber?'

'That's what I said. I find a reference to this person, a German national, in the documents I referred to. With me when making my search I had the assistance of a detective inspector from Scotland Yard. This policeman was able to tell me that a certain Otto Leber had been found dead aboard this ship in the port of Liverpool, after committing murder. This person was a known spy, a dirty occupation if ever there was one. Very un-British, but then of course he was a blasted German, so what can you expect? I repeat my question, Senhor Peixoto: do you know this person, this spy?'

'Certainly I do not, and I must—'

'One moment.' Watkiss held up a commanding hand. 'You're aware, I think, that another body was found, disintegrated, in the cable locker aboard the *Taronga Park*. It has been established that this was that of a female, and that her name was Peixoto. Maria Peixoto, Senhor.' After a pause he added, 'Your niece.'

Peixoto's eyes blazed. 'I do not believe this!'

'It happens to be a fact, Senhor—'

'You cannot prove anything.'

'Oh, yes, I can,' Watkiss stated. 'I have the written depositions of the British consul in Santarem, who was party to all the filth that you were organizing. I say that with respect, of course, since you are after all the minister to whom I'm responsible. I trust you've been

272

paying attention to what I've been saying, Captain von Grützner?'

'Yes—'

'Excellent! I have some more to say, so you'll continue listening. It's a blasted pity Colonel de Souza's too damn ignorant to speak English, but the whole thing'll be translated into da—Portuguese eventually. Yes, what is it, Mr Mayhew?'

Mayhew hissed at him. 'Really, this cannot be allowed to continue—all the requirements of diplomacy suggest—'

'They can suggest what they blasted well like, Mr Mayhew, I shall continue nevertheless—'

'Can you not think even of your own position, Admiral?'

'I put my duty first,' Watkiss said with simple dignity, 'and it's a blasted disgrace that *you* don't. Now kindly hold your tongue.' He paused; all eyes were on him now; Halfhyde made no move to interfere. Watkiss continued, 'I am in possession of all the evidence necessary to show that Millington accepted bribes from Senhor Peixoto personally to falsify his despatches to London in regard to the true purpose of the German base; he had kept all the documents intact, no doubt so that he would have some kind of a hold upon yourself, Senhor Peixoto, should you try to renege. What have you to say to this, may I ask, Senhor?'

There was no reply.

273

Watkiss went on triumphantly, 'I thought as much! You played for high stakes and you blasted well made a balls of it, didn't you? And there was the personal angle, was there not? *You* had a hold upon poor Millington on account of the jiggery-pokery with your niece, Marie, whom you—'

'I did not kill her!' Peixoto shouted, his fists clenched.

'Quite, I know that. I never said you did, did I? It was Millington who killed her—or rather, arranged for her to be killed—'

'You can prove this?'

'No, I can't,' Watkiss said with honesty. 'It is what that policeman Todhunter calls circumstantial evidence, am I not right, Todhunter?'

'Yes, sir, quite right. In certain circumstances, such evidence can be produced before a jury and—'

'Yes, yes, thank you, Todhunter, that'll do. Just repeat in front of Senhor Peixoto what you said to me earlier.'

'About what, sir?'

'Oh, for goodness' sake, Todhunter, about Senhor Peixoto!'

'Oh, yes, sir.' Todhunter brought out a notebook, and, with licked thumb, leafed through the pages. 'I said, sir, Senhor Peixoto would do himself a favour, sir, if he was to keep his trap shut, Mr Millington being already

274

dead, sir—'

'Yes, well, we'll leave that part, thank you, Todhunter. Simply advance your reconstruction.'

'I didn't make a note of that, sir. It was only—'

'Oh, bugger your notes, Todhunter, try to blasted well remember, can't you?'

'Very good, sir.' Todhunter closed his eyes for a moment, thinking back, since it was important to get it absolutely right. He tried to imagine himself far, far across the seas, in London, giving evidence before My Lords the Queen's Justices in the Central Criminal Court, a very different kettle of fish from the stenches of Santarem and a load of foreign gentlemen with greasy brownish skins and moustaches like brigands. 'My reconstruction, sir, yes. Well, sir and you gentlemen, my reconstruction, my hypothesis, went like this.' He gave a cough, and as he did so he saw Halfhyde move across the cabin to stand between Senhor Peixoto and Admiral Watkiss. 'Mr Millington, who had been having an, er, affair with Miss Maria Peixoto and not wishing this to become public knowledge on account of his particular position in regard to both the British and the—'

'Oh, cut the blasted verbiage, Todhunter!'

'Yes, sir, I do apologize, I do really. Mr Millington, then, decided upon murder, his passion having cooled—'

'Because,' Watkiss interposed to save time, 'he was keener on becoming a very rich man.'

'Yes, sir, just so. Just so.' Mr Todhunter's memory had missed a beat but only temporarily. 'Thus he arranged for Otto Leber, a German, to carry out the murder on his behalf. It might be asked, I think, why Miss Peixoto had gone aboard the *Taronga Park*. My hypothesis is this, sir and other gentlemen.' He coughed again, apologetically. 'Otto Leber, to whom she was known—that much is documented—lured her aboard, he being about to indulge in chicanery on the ship, you see, and took advantage of her proximity, as aforethought of course, and thereafter—'

'Thank you, Todhunter.' Watkiss clicked his tongue. 'What he means is, this wretched fellow Leber killed the woman and bunged her through the inspection hatch into the cable locker, not thinking the remains would ever be found—the violent movement of the cable when let go, you see. I think that holds water well enough. An unfortunate end I must say.'

Peixoto found his voice. 'Where do I come into this stupid hypothesis, Admiral?'

Watkiss shrugged. 'You do not, Senhor, in a direct sense. But it is possible you got to hear of the murder of your niece, for whom I dare say you had affection. Whatever the reason, Senhor Peixoto, I believe you arranged for Millington to be slaughtered by your blasted brigand,

276

handy in Santarem, under the guise of a mob attack on the British consulate—and by God you're not going to slide out from under that!'

A fraction of a second later Admiral Watkiss gave a loud cry and jumped into the air. Blood appeared on his white tunic. 'By God, Mr Halfhyde, I'm wounded! The bugger's blasted well killed me I fancy—'

Peixoto had been fast; Halfhyde had been faster. He said, 'You're not dead yet sir.'

'Oh.'

Halfhyde bent and picked up a thin, very sharp knife. Peixoto was clasping his wrist and groaning with pain. Colonel de Souza, who hadn't understood a word, was looking totally uncertain as to what he should do, so did nothing but wave his arms excitedly. Admiral Watkiss, deciding to look martyred until someone produced a bandage, resumed his accusations since he had not finished yet. He turned to Captain von Grützner.

'Captain, Millington's documents contain certain very important references to your base, very damaging to your blasted Emperor I might add. German gold changed hands ... some of it towards Millington, a great deal more to Senhor Peixoto. Rio de Janeiro is a long way from Santarem, is it not, and communications are poor. Besides, Senhor Peixoto was respected and trusted by his President ... to be brief, Captain von Grützner, as you well know the

277

Brazilian government as such had no blasted knowledge of what your trading post was in fact intended for—even the local dignitaries had been bribed to hold their tongues, while of course the lesser fry are all illiterate anyway—and they wouldn't have known until the submarine base had become a physical fact. At which time, there is a suggestion that Senhor Peixoto would have attempted a military *coup d'état* against his President. All this is *amply* supported by poor Millington's papers.' Watkiss turned aside to Halfhyde. 'It's why the buggers in Rio didn't confide in me—they could scarcely confide what they didn't damn well know!'

'No indeed, sir.'

Watkiss addressed the German again. 'My dear sir, the Brazilian government had *no wish* for a warlike base to be established, and now all this has been blown into the open, your blasted Emperor will be thrown out lock, stock and blasted barrel...'

vi

'A message,' Admiral Watkiss said later, when matters had been explained to Colonel de Souza by Mayhew and the Minister for Army and Marine had been arrested and taken away, 'will go at once to the Admiralty via the cable station at Georgetown in British Guiana. It'll take time, of course.' He wiped at his face; it had been an

278

exhausting morning. 'In the meantime I'll have been in touch with Rio de Janeiro and that Hun will get his marching orders you may be sure. Now—what about you?'

'My job's done, sir. I shall return to Liverpool after taking bunkers in the Demerara River.'

'Yes. Damn it, my dear Halfhyde, I shall be sorry to see you go, very sorry, and that's something I never thought I'd ever say. But it's the fact. These blasted dagoes, and their dreadful climate! Didn't some blasted poet once write something about oh to be in England now that April's here?'

'It's not April, sir—'

'Oh, balls and bang me arse, there you go again, you never change—splitting hairs! I know it's damn well not April! But surely you understand? A sight of the dockyard at Portsmouth ... the church of St Thomas, the Round Tower, Fort Blockhouse, the South Railway jetty. All those splendid battleships.' Admiral Watkiss appeared to be on the verge of tears.

'I understand, sir, very well indeed. Indeed I was wondering...'

'Yes, Mr Halfhyde?'

'Perhaps it would be advisable for you to remain aboard and return with me.'

'To England?' Watkiss stared, mouth dropping open.

279

'A question of your personal safety, sir.'

'Oh no, that's balls, my dear fellow, though decent of you to be sure ... I'm perfectly safe. I've blown the gaff about a blasted dago traitor and the other dagoes will be grateful. One can't have bribery and corruption.'

'But the Brazilians—'

'Oh, I know what you mean, Mr Halfhyde. An appalling lot! But I'm an admiral, you know.' Watkiss sounded almost pathetic. 'That's not something I can give up easily—I'm an honoured person out here in this blasted country, with a splendid residence in Rio de Janeiro, and servants by the score. If I went back to England I'd not be so honoured, I fear. The blasted Admiralty never really appreciated me, I'm sorry to say.'

'A prophet in his own country, sir—'

'Yes, yes, he's never honoured. I'm glad you agree, Mr Halfhyde, very glad indeed.'

Shortly after, Admiral Watkiss took his leave; Halfhyde went down to the gangway to bid him Godspeed. As he went over the side Watkiss looked up at the Master's deck and saw Victoria leaning over the rail. He paused. 'That woman, Mr Halfhyde. What do you propose to do with her?'

Halfhyde smiled. 'What would you propose to do with a woman, sir?'

'There's no need to be vulgar, Mr Halfhyde.' Admiral Watkiss turned away down the

280

gangway and proceeded along the jetty, a squat figure with shorts a-flap and telescope held like a truncheon, bouncing with rapid steps towards shelter as, once again, the rains broke and within seconds drenched him from head to foot.

Photoset, printed and bound in Great Britain by
REDWOOD PRESS LIMITED, Melksham, Wiltshire